Other Clarion novels by Stella Pevsner

Lindsay, Lindsay, Fly Away Home

STELLA PEVSNER

Lindsay, Lindsay, Fly Away Home

CLARION BOOKS

TICKNOR & FIELDS: A HOUGHTON MIFFLIN COMPANY

NEW YORK

Clarion Books
Ticknor & Fields, a Houghton Mifflin Company

Library of Congress Cataloging in Publication Data
Pevsner, Stella.
    Lindsay, Lindsay, fly away home.
    Summary: Teenaged Lindsay, after spending most of her
life in India and other faraway places, is unwilling to
adjust to living and going to school in the United States.
    [1. Moving, Household—Fiction] I. Title.
PZ7.P44815Li 1983   [Fic]   83–2115
ISBN 0–89919–186–X

S 10 9 8 7 6 5 4 3 2 1

For my nieces and nephews . . .
who have added an extra
dimension of love to my life

Chapter One

I knew the rest of the flight was going to be bloody awful the minute all those kids swarmed aboard the plane in Paris. They came stampeding down the aisles, bleating to one another like a herd of goats and cramming unbelievable amounts of belongings into every available space.

"American teenagers," someone behind me said. "Oh lord, why this particular flight?"

"It must be the spring break," the other person said. "They used to go to Florida. Now they go to Europe."

I held my breath, hoping no one had been assigned the two seats next to me, but then I saw the stewardess point in my direction and sure enough, two girls shuffled forward. The first one, wide as a door, kept saying cheerfully, "Sorry, sorry," as the bags hanging all over her bumped into shoulders. At my row she lowered some of her freight to the floor. "You shove in first, Krissy-baby," she said to the other girl. "I like the aisle seat so I can cut loose for some action."

Grudgingly, I moved my purse and sweater and managed a "That's okay," when the second girl said she was sorry. There was another awkward moment when I leaned down to move my overnight bag just as she was swinging hers to the floor. "I'm really sorry," she said.

I shrugged. "It's your space. Are you on a school excursion?"

"Yes. To Paris. Well, back from, now. I'm Krissy." She had a sweet smile, and was pretty in an ordinary sort of way.

"I'm Lindsay."

Krissy touched the arm of the other girl, who was about to get up. "Bones, this is Lindsay."

The heavy girl nodded. "Hey, how ya doin'." She hoisted herself into the aisle, stripped off what I later learned was a windbreaker, wadded it and poked it into the already packed overhead storage. Yanking down a T-shirt . . . she really was *big* . . . the girl said, "Kid, I'm going to the john. If you see Ape-Face, tell him to start shuffling. The game's still on."

"Please sit down and fasten your seat belt," a stewardess, materializing from behind, ordered.

Bones tucked the end of her T-shirt into her jeans. "Hey, lady, give me a break, will you? I'm just going to the powder room. *La salle de . . .* what's the word, Kris?"

"Please take your seat. We are moving to position." The attendant waited until the girl, with a huge sigh, dropped back into the seat and fastened her seat belt.

"*Merde,*" Bones muttered. "You'd think we were back in that stinkin' *ecole.*"

"Bones," Krissy said in an undertone. "She's French, you know."

"That cuts no ice with me." Bones leaned forward a bit and peered at me. "Is there some other school aboard? That you're with?"

"I'm traveling alone." And then to be polite, I added, "What school are you with?"

"Hemingway High. We were runner-up at the state finals last year. Right, Krissy?"

"Right." And to me, "We missed by only one point."

"Oh. Smashing." I hadn't a clue of what they were talking about.

"And where do you hail from?" Bones was still looking me over.

"Uh . . . oh . . . well, the American School. In India."

It was a bit unnerving, the way she stared at me as she repeated, "The American School. In India."

Something more seemed to be called for. "My father's in international business, so we've moved about quite a lot. Hong Kong, Germany, France . . . and for quite a while now, India."

"Hey, that's wild. So how's come you're going to the States?"

I really didn't want to go into it. "Some friends of ours moved back last fall." That obviously wasn't enough, so I improvised. "My parents want me to . . . experience life in the States. Before college, you know. So I'm going to live with my aunt for a while."

"Oh, man, I'll bet my folks would like to ship me off somewhere," Bones said. "Siberia, for starters. Right, Kris? And some teachers, too, I could name but won't, what with their radar hearing." Bones cocked a thumb toward the back of the plane.

"How long were you in Paris?" I asked.

"Ten days," Krissy said, picking at her nail polish. "It seems like a month."

"Ha!" Bones shot out. "That's because lover boy wasn't on the trip." Across Krissy she said to me, "The kid here really has the hots for old Neimeyer." And back to Krissy, "Admit it, kid. You know you'd do anything for J.C., and I mean anything. Am I right or am I right?"

"Oh . . . *fermez*." With reddened face, Krissy picked up her purse and took out an emery board.

I turned, from embarrassment, to look out the window. We had made a turn and the pilot, over the intercom, seemed to be explaining our position in line, but it was impossible, with all the hubbub, to sort out the exact words. Earlier I had felt tired and a bit apprehensive about this total change about to take place in my life. Now I felt decidedly depressed. Was I destined to muck about for months with the likes of these kids, or was this group just abnormally rowdy?

By the time we were aloft things had quieted down a bit. The attendants began pushing refreshment carts down the aisles, and with set smiles were handing out soft drinks. Kris and I both took 7-Ups but Bones put in a request for beer and got it.

"You're crazy," Kris said.

"Hey, it's legal, as long as we don't touch land. . . ."

"Not if Miss Pritchard sees you, it's not."

"Relax. I saw the whole bunch of teachers in the back when I finally made it to the john. They're all zonked out. Tough trip." She hoisted herself forward. "Hold the fort while I go over and play a few rounds. Bones is my name and poker's my game."

I waited until she was out of earshot to ask, "Is that really her name?"

"No, it's Selma," Kris said. "But she likes to be called Bones because that reminds her they're in there somewhere."

"I wonder that she doesn't diet."

"She says she would, only there's no food she's willing to give up." Krissy began the nervous habit of picking at her polish again. "It's hard to give up anything, I guess. Food, cigarettes, booze . . . boyfriend."

I gave her a glance. She was biting her lips now. "He's

going out with someone else. My boyfriend. I thought the trip would make me forget, but you know, every time we were in some great place like Notre Dame or the Eiffel Tower I'd find myself thinking, *If only Jimmy were here, I could really enjoy this*. It was like, you know, he was on my mind even more than at home." She looked at my hands and I realized I was twisting the ring.

"Are you ... uh ... engaged?" she quietly asked.

I had to keep myself from covering the star sapphire. I'd carried it around for some time now but put it on only when I got onto the plane. "It's not ... well, really not an engagement ring. Although actually it *is* from my friend."

"In India?"

"Yes. He happens to be Indian. His name is Rajee."

"Oh." Her tone had no emotion.

"And you know how it is. There's no prejudice on either side, but 'Wouldn't you be happier, sticking to your own kind, my dear?'"

"Your parents?"

"Well, my father. And he ... Rajee ... was positively bucking his own caste system by showing attention to an alien. His family is quite wealthy."

"That's terrible. I mean that parents stood in your way."

"That's life." I sighed. "So now I'm being shipped off to the relief of all the elders. *C'est formidable*."

"Well, as soon as you're eighteen you'll be your own boss. Then there's nothing they can do about anything."

"Oh, true. But in the meantime ..." I gave a rather dramatic sigh. I was beginning to enjoy this.

"My mother's a real dragon sometimes," Krissy said. "But still ..."

"Yes. Well, you see, my real mother is dead."

"Ohhhh." Krissy gave me a look. "I'm sorry."

"It happened a long time ago. I was a little kid at the time. But then a few years ago, when we lived in Paris, my father finally remarried. She's French."

"Really. Do you get along with her?"

"Famously. Claudine's young and pretty and has a great deal of spirit. She's more like an older sister, actually. She wasn't entirely a good influence on me; everyone thought that. And it's true, I admit. It caused scenes between Claudine and my father — her letting me get by with things."

"Hey, no kidding. Like what?"

"When I was about ten, Claudine allowed me to wear makeup, like a film star, to school, until the teachers brought it to father's attention. But lately it's been my hanging about with Rajee that caused the big fuss. Father claimed that Claudine encouraged us, which, of course, she did, being a romantic herself. The French are so reasonable about affairs of the heart. Claudine thought it perfectly natural that I be in love at my age."

"She sounds great. Do you have a picture of her?"

"Yes, just here, I'll show you." I pulled the plastic photo section from my wallet. "That's Claudine."

Kris looked at it and smiled. "Oh, she's darling. Is this recent?"

"Fairly. Here's my father."

"Nice looking. He reminds me of an actor in a foreign legion film. That type."

"So he does. Stiff upper lip and all that." I flipped to another photo. "Here's Rajee. And me. Jess took this last year in the Mogul Gardens."

"You make a really nice-looking couple. His dark hair and eyes and your strawberry-blond and . . ." she looked at me. "Blue eyes. Who's Jess?"

6

"Jess is my lifelong friend. Literally. His parents and mine have been all over the world together. See, here he is."

"Oh, he's *really* cute!" And then, catching herself, she said, "I mean . . . cute in a different way from . . . from Rajee. How old is he?"

"Just seventeen. Jess and his parents are back in the States. They came over last fall."

"Yeh? How does he like the good old USA?"

"All right, but he misses me dreadfully. We've shared so many adventures, you know. Our fathers work together, so we've always moved together."

"Until now, right?"

"Right." I sighed. "It will be quite a comfort to Jess to have me around. Someone who understands. He does have a sister, but she's an absolute ninny."

"How old is she?"

"Ruthanne? About fourteen. Oh, here comes Selma." I put the photos back into my purse. "Is the game over, then?" I asked.

"Yeh. Those guys tried paying off in francs." She settled into her seat. "What's going on?"

Krissy said, "Lindsay's been telling me about . . . India. I just love Lindsay's accent. Don't you, Bones? Don't you just love Lindsay's accent?"

Bones was rummaging through the stuff in the seat pocket in front of her. "Yes. I just love Lindsay's accent. Aha, here's the barf bag. Gotta keep this sucker handy. That beer didn't set so good."

Krissy went on. "Freshman year we had a girl from Australia at our school. Remember her, Bones? Everyone was crazy about her accent. Especially the guys."

"They were crazy about more than her accent."

"She lost it in a year or two, though. Right, Bones?"

"She lost it, all right. About the accent, I'm not so sure."

Krissy poked her with an elbow. "Now stop that. Anyway, Lindsay, you're bound to be very popular."

"That's really not important to me, you know." Neither girl looked as though she believed me. I wasn't sure that *I* believed me. "Actually, I'm afraid it will be a bit of a bother, explaining to all that I'm an American subject." I could feel the British accent really taking over. "An expatriate I believe it's called. And I have acquired certain habits and customs. Just now, for instance, I feel a decided need to meditate." I paused. "Would you mind terribly if I lit a bit of incense as an aid to relaxation?"

Kris looked bewildered. "But where . . . ?"

From my purse I extracted a sandalwood-scented cone. "Just here in the ashtray." I put it onto the little snub-out thing and held a match to it.

"But the smoking section . . ."

"Starts right behind us. They've been puffing away like the devil's own, without the least regard . . ." I breathed deeply as the fumes curled. "Oh, isn't this heaven. It brings back so many memories. . . ."

It also brought the attendant. Before she reached us, I'd snapped the lid shut and blown away the smoke. She paused, looked perplexed, and moved on.

After dinner and the movie the passengers settled down for a few winks. Bones, with her seat tilted back practically onto the lap of the person behind, fell into a snoring slumber. Krissy punched a pillow into the seat division and seemed to be sleeping. Too nervous to settle down, I pulled Jess's letter from my purse. It was an old one, from last November, but a favorite. He'd never been so open since. Too painful, I expect. I folded it down to the best paragraph:

> ... *lonesome at times. There's no one around that I can say, "Remember when" to and know that they'll know what I mean. Sometimes I wish there really were magic carpets floating around up there. I'd hail one and say, "Take me to Bombay." And then I'd be with you and maybe we'd talk about the times we saw the Taj Mahal. Remember? You're the only person in the whole world who knows what it was like that day when we first saw it. Kids around here* ...

And then he went on about how American kids knew little about India and cared less, so he learned not to go on about it. But he said half the time he didn't know what the kids were talking about ... like sports events that had taken place in the past, or famous people he'd never even heard of. They used brand names a lot, too, and slang terms, and told inside jokes.

Well, Jess, I thought, even though you haven't gone on about it lately, you must still feel an outsider. When I get there we'll stand together and form our own little culture club. I won't even try to blend in because the past is too much a part of me. I *want* to remember.

And suddenly, sitting there, I knew exactly the thing that would say it all to Jess the minute we met, without any actual words being said. After we cleared customs in New York, and before I rechecked my luggage I'd take it out. The sari. And then, just before the fasten-your-seat-belt sign came on for the Chicago landing, I'd duck into the loo and wrap myself in the outfit. No matter that I'd brought it for Ruthanne. . . . She could have the bronze buddha instead. I'd greet Jess at the airport looking every inch the maharani. I'd even put a bright red lipstick dot on my forehead.

Suddenly the apprehension over the new life and new surroundings vanished. I'd greet them in style. . . . Show dear old Aunt Meg exactly what she'd landed as a live-in house guest. Whatever Dad had written to her and warned her of in advance wouldn't matter a bit. Wherever I was I'd still be me, with nothing changed: Jess would know that the minute he laid eyes on me. He'd be so pleased!

Chapter Two

Aunt Meg was something of a mystery to me. You'd think, as Dad's only sibling (and nearest relative, too, since their parents were no longer living), that she'd be close in spirit though distance separated them. Such was not the case.

Meg wrote a letter now and then, but had never popped over for a visit the way other kids' relatives sometimes did. And toward me, her one and only niece, she showed little interest or even curiosity. When she did write to father he'd put the letter away and say something like, "Your Aunt Meg sends her fondest."

Fondness be damned. I'd have preferred something more material, like American clothes or gadgets. It was hard to keep an air of indifference when other kids were showing off loot from the Colonies, as some British people still called the States.

I once asked Father why Aunt Meg never came across with a gift, even on my birthday, and he just spluttered and looked a bit embarrassed, as well he might, having a skinflint for a sister.

Lately, though, there had been telephone conversations. How many I didn't know, since they always seemed to occur when I wasn't around. The only reason I know about them was because once Claudine remarked that Aunt

Meg's hours had been changed at work so she'd be home most of the time when I got out of school.

Actually, I knew more about Aunt Meg from Ruthanne's letters than anything else. It seemed to me that Ruthanne had a schoolgirl crush on my aunt. *So sophisticated,* she'd said in that last letter. *The kids at school just can't believe that I know Meg of the* Meg and Murray Show. *I had to get her autograph to prove it to some of them.* Big thrills that was. I'd hardly place someone in the celebrity class simply because of a radio show.

"Claudine," I'd asked, after reading Ruthanne's letter, "how does it happen we have no pictures of this Aunt Meg person?"

Claudine shrugged. "Perhaps your father would like to forget . . ."

"What? That she's his sister? Really, now."

I could always read Claudine like a book. That day I could tell she was uneasy by the way she raked her fingers through her hair.

I kept at it. "What is there about Meg that Father would like to forget? That she's good-looking, talented, and has a terrific job? Eh?"

"Of course she is truly wonderful, this virgin princess, Meg." Claudine got up abruptly, tightened the belt of her kimono, and knelt before the record player to select an album.

"Why do you say *virgin* princess? Wasn't Meg married at one time?"

"Oh, yes," Claudine said, putting a record on the turntable. "Let us not forget the marriage."

"Marriage? Who's getting married?" Father asked, coming into the room. Claudine's hand seemed caught in the air, like a stilled butterfly.

"One of the servants," I said. "A relative of one of the servants."

"Oh." He started across the room. "I'm going to shower."

Claudine looked like a child who had been reprieved from punishment. Why? I wondered. What was it all about, this conspiracy of silence?

Except in the most general way, Father avoided any explanation of Aunt Meg. Yet he was shipping his one and only daughter into her tender care. It didn't make sense. I gave up and tried not to dwell on it.

But now, with the plane about to land, I felt decidedly nervous. My hand actually trembled as I sat there in my sari, trying to get a perfect dot on my forehead with the bright red lipstick Krissy let me use for the purpose.

To my immense relief, the kids around me took little notice of my garb. They were too caught up with the idea of seeing friends and family once again.

I sat waiting when the other passengers shoved forward toward the exit doors. For one thing, if I got caught in a crush my sari would probably come unwound. For another, I rather liked the idea of drifting out alone and making a grand impression.

When I did move through the tunnel toward the waiting room my heart started going thumpity-thump. What if Aunt Meg were there all alone!

The first person I saw was Jess. Taller than ever, he was. Freckled as ever, too. His face lit up at the sight of me and he rushed forward to give me a great hug that almost lifted me off my feet. Then Ruthanne brushed her brother aside and hugged me. "Oh, Lindsay, I'm so glad to see you!" She lowered her arms and added, "But why are you in costume? Oh, here's Mom."

Still another hug. Then Mrs. McIntyre (Aunt Janice

I'd always called her) turned and touched the woman standing beside her. "And here, Lindsay, is your aunt Meg."

My heart lurched. This was the moment, then. I'd never really pictured Meg as a *person*. Nervous as I was, I saw that she in turn looked positively petrified.

There was a tiny suspension of time in which she was probably wondering, as was I, whether a kiss was in order. I solved it, though, by holding out my hand. Hers was icy cold. She was younger looking than I'd expected. Slim, rather elegant, with dark blond hair cut in such a way that it swung forward as she moved.

"Welcome, Lindsay," she said. And then, "Your plane was right on time."

Such an ordinary observation from someone almost famous.

"Here, let me take your stuff," Jess said, picking up my tote bag. "You travel light, compared to the bunch of kids that just got off."

"Tourists," I said.

"You don't have a coat," Aunt Janice commented. "Better put on that sweater you're carrying."

"But it's April. It should be hot."

"Not here," Jess said. "Not yet."

"We'll have to get you some things," Aunt Meg said with a smile. "Good excuse for a shopping spree." Her lighthearted words bore no real relation to the rather mesmerized look on her face.

"Well!" Aunt Janice said, taking charge. "On to the baggage department. Come along, all." She took Aunt Meg's arm, as they went ahead, and said something. Aunt Meg nodded.

People were crowded all about us, bumping around

14

with their bags. It was a job making our way down the passage. At least, though, passengers along with friends and family weren't lounging about on the floor as they have a way of doing in the Indian airports.

Ruthanne was babbling as usual, mostly about the wonderfulness of Aunt Meg, and saying I was so lucky to be about to get new clothes.

"I have plenty of things," I told Ruthanne. "What does Meg think . . . that I always go around in a sari?"

"Since you mention it," Jess said, "why *are* you dressed like this?"

I could tell straightaway that rather than being pleased, Jess was just a tad disapproving.

"Some kids on the plane talked me into it as a bit of a lark," I said quickly. "And I thought it would be a nice surprise for you, to bring back memories."

Jess merely grunted.

"Don't worry about it, Lindsay," Ruthanne said. "We're not likely to meet anyone we know."

There was another great bit of commotion getting my bags and making our way to the car. I was distinctly shocked when Jess got into the driver's seat. No kid in India is allowed to drive that young. I started to get in beside him but Ruthanne coaxed me to sit next to her in the back, with Aunt Meg. I was in the middle in more ways than one. Everyone was shooting questions at me. I felt almost like weeping.

"We shouldn't be bombarding you like this," Aunt Meg said, showing a sensitivity I wouldn't have expected. "The flight must have been exhausting. And now finding yourself in a new place . . ."

With an aunt you barely know, she should have added. "Yes, I am a bit weary," I said.

15

"We'll get you home, give you a snack, and then get you into bed," Aunt Meg went on. "It's lucky this flight got in in the evening. And that it's Friday."

What did Friday have to do with anything?

"Just wait until you hear Aunt Meg on the air!" Ruthanne said. "She's dynamite." So she was called *Aunt Meg* by all.

Meg laughed. "Oh, Ruthanne, I'm not. And it's nothing to be so excited about. It's only a job."

"Don't say that! The kids think it's fab! And so do I!"

Already, Ruthanne was getting on my nerves. "How far do you live from the airport?" I asked Aunt Meg, just to change the subject.

"About twenty minutes. We'll be home before you know it."

Home. Hers maybe, but not mine. Ever.

I didn't see Jess and Ruthanne's father that night because he was at a meeting. (Uncle Robert and my father were always at meetings or out of town or out of the country it seemed.) Ruthanne wanted to hang about when we got to the house but her mother insisted they leave as soon as Jess brought in my baggage. "You can catch up on the talk tomorrow," she said. "Lindsay has got to get to bed, poor thing."

In a way, I was wishing they'd stay for a bit so I could avoid having to talk to my aunt. I must admit she was being nice, though. While I sat at the kitchen table like some sort of zombie, she put out food and talked some, but not too much, and about general things.

In my room . . . and I was going to change a few things *there* when I had my strength back . . . she asked if I wanted her to help me unpack.

"Not now," I told her. "It can wait."

"But your pajamas . . . ?"

"I don't have any."

"Oh. Then a nightgown."

"I haven't one of those either."

"But then . . . ?"

"I sleep in the raw," I told her. "Nature's own." I don't know why I said all that. A bit of contrariness in my nature, I expect.

She blinked but merely said, "Good night."

"Good night."

Again there was that hesitation as she continued to stand there. Why should I kiss her good night, though? This stranger was less familiar to me than the servants back home.

"It will be good to get into bed," I said, unwrapping the sari. "I'm really most dreadfully tired."

"I'll bet you are. Sleep as long as you like tomorrow. Well, good night again."

The minute she closed the door I yanked off the clothes, dropped them on the floor, and flopped into bed. I felt I could easily sleep for two days at least.

But sleep didn't come. My body ached with fatigue. I twisted and turned. Confused images darted through my mind, and snatches of talk. My *ayah* weeping and lamenting, "Oh, what I do when *Baba* Lindsay go so far away, never see loving *ayah* no more?"

And the voices from the verandah late at night . . . Father and Claudine laughing sometimes, but more often lately, quarreling, Claudine's voice thick with drink. And Rajee . . . our last meeting when his gorgeous brown eyes were filled with sadness and desolation. The ring . . . Rajee had given me the ring. I held it to my lips now and kissed it . . . as he had when he put it on my finger. Star sapphire . . . symbol of undying love.

Somewhere along the line I drifted off. When I woke and looked at the clock by my bed it was some time after four. I did this on and off, sleeping drowsily, and then suddenly waking.

Once I became aware of the door being open and then a figure . . . Aunt Meg . . . standing there.

"Wh . . . what?" I lifted my head.

"Oh, nothing. Are you okay?"

"Okay? Yes . . . why . . . ?"

"You were calling out in your sleep."

"Oh." I flopped down again and yawned. "I do that sometimes." Yawn. "Sorry . . ." Yawn.

"You're just overtired. Good night, Lindsay." Gently, she closed the door. I wondered how long she'd been standing there, gazing at me . . . and for whom I'd been calling. Father? Claudine? Rajee? Or had I slipped way back to my early childhood and called out for my poor dead mother? I used to get most upset by those dreams. But now if I cried there was no *ayah* to come and cuddle me.

No matter. Sleep, now, was all that mattered. I was so dreadfully tired.

Ruthanne was sitting at the kitchen table talking to Aunt Meg when I wandered out the next day. "Well, here you are at last, sleepyhead," she said. "Know what time it is?"

"Haven't the foggiest."

Ruthanne pointed to the wall clock. "Two P.M. You really crashed." She talked with an American accent, I

18

noticed. And *crashed.* "How do you feel? Is it okay if I bring some friends over? They're dying to meet you."

"Oh, honey," Aunt Meg said. "Let Lindsay get acclimated first, why don't you? I doubt that she's up to meeting new people just now."

Aunt Meg was behaving all right so far. But who could tell what she had in mind? I'd read an article in an American journal about how experts deprogrammed kids who'd got caught up in cults. Was she planning to deprogram me where Rajee was concerned?

"So, honey," Aunt Meg was going on with Ruthanne, "would you just postpone the introductions for a while?"

"Oh, sure. Sorry. I'm just so excited."

"And now, Lindsay, what may I get for you? Eggs? Cereal? Sandwich?"

At least she wasn't giving me that *honey* business.

"Just toast and tea, please. I never eat much before I meditate."

Ruthanne burst out laughing. "Oh, Lindsay, you still haven't changed!"

I stared at her. Then, coldly, "I can't see what you find so amusing." Why did this beastly child have to be here, making me feel discomfited in front of my relative?

"Well, actually," Ruthanne said, "it isn't the meditating that's so funny. It's just that your saying it reminded me of the time you ran away and joined the *ashram.*"

"That wasn't particularly amusing either."

Ruthanne turned. "Aunt Meg, did you know about Lindsay and the *ashram?* It was wild. She said she was going to shave her head and put on the orange robe and join the cult. Only her dad dragged her away before she could do anything."

I wished someone would drag Ruthanne away.

Aunt Meg gave a little laugh, as though the whole thing was just an amusing story. "Any particular kind of bread?" she asked me.

"Uh . . . any kind."

"Of course. You're probably still deep in jet lag, and here I am, asking for choices." She put on the water to heat. "I'll just serve and be quiet."

I asked Ruthanne what Jess was doing.

"He's at work. At the car wash."

"The what?"

"Car wash. Oh, Lindsay . . . !"

Aunt Meg broke in smoothly, "It's a mechanical thing. Cars are pulled by chains through jets of water. Then they have kids at the other end to wipe off the windshields and chrome trim." She put dishes and silver in front of me and got out the bread. "Ruthanne, would you mind leaving Lindsay and me alone for a while? We have so many things to discuss in private."

"Oh, sure. I know how it is." She got up and gave Meg a peck on the cheek. "Then see you later, Lindsay."

"Right." I braced myself but she left without touching me.

Pausing until Ruthanne was gone, Aunt Meg said, "Sorry about that little fib. Ruthanne's a sweet child but there are times . . ."

"Don't I know."

"Really, I need to go out on errands and I thought you'd rather be alone for a while."

"Quite right. I still feel rather tired."

"Of course you do. Now, please make yourself at home. The house is yours to explore and to settle into, whenever you feel up to it."

"Yes, well, all right."

She put the tea and toast in front of me, along with butter and jam. Her hand tentatively touched my shoulder. I could look up and invite affection if I chose. I stiffened instead.

I must admit I felt the tiniest bit of contrition as Meg left, but then what did she expect? She might be my blood aunt but I felt ever so much closer to Aunt Janice, who was, in fact, not a relative at all.

Buttering the toast and heaping it with jam, I wondered a bit about Aunt Janice and whether or not she knew why I'd been sent here. She probably did. . . . She was like a big, commonsense sister to Claudine . . . but she was one of those women who didn't exactly confide in kids. Jess might know, though, through Uncle Robert, who was less guarded. (He was the type of adult who assumed children believed what they were told, and didn't hear what they weren't supposed to hear.) I'd ask Jess what sort of talk he'd overhead, if any.

I felt fairly certain, though, that sending me here was an elaborate scheme to get me away from Rajee. Dear Rajee, so heartbroken at my leaving. "You will have so many grand adventures in the United States," he'd told me at our last meeting. "But I will be left only with sad memories."

"Sad?"

"Yes, sad, because you will no longer be here to share them." He had wept a bit. Rajee was most sentimental.

I'd left him with the promise of returning as soon as I could. "Don't forget," I told him, "when I'm eighteen I'll be able to do as I please. No one will separate us then."

In a little while I'd write to him, repeating that promise. In the meantime, though, before *she* got back, I'd have a look about this prison. Finishing the tea I thought, I'm a bit like one of the wives of Henry the Eighth, sent off to the tower for the terrible crime of falling in love. There were differences, of course, but the idea was the same: People who fall in love inappropriately are treated in a most cruel way. I would survive, though. Somehow I would survive!

Chapter Three

Looking around the kitchen, I had no way of knowing whether Aunt Meg was wealthy or if this was standard American. There did seem to be a frightful array of appliances. Back home, with all the servants, there was no need for such things.

I wandered out to a verandah with its screens and mat flooring and white wicker furniture. Quite nice, as a matter of fact. The fat cushions were covered in a tropical design of yellow and green. Back in the house proper I wandered through a room with a beige leathery sofa and chairs and a TV with a big blank screen. I hoped that here, at least, one could get a variety of programs in the English language, and films that didn't all date back to the thirties. At the other end of this room was a dining area with a rather attractive glass oval table and brass chairs with velvet upholstery.

There was still another room . . . the parlor, it seemed to be. What use had Aunt Meg for all these rooms? This one was done in tones of gray and coral. Quite tasteful, actually. I recognized several decorative pieces that must have been sent by Father from Bangkok or perhaps Hong Kong.

There were three bedrooms, one with its own bath. The bath leading off the hall was for servants, I supposed, although I hadn't seen any about so far.

I went into the largest bedroom, the one with its own bath. *Her* room, naturally. Claudine's, back in India, was always in a jumble, even with people about to tidy up after her. Meg's room, though, had nothing lying about. The bed looked enormous for one person, and the side tables were bare except for lamps and books and an ashtray. I walked over and picked up a book. From the title and photo it seemed to be some actress's biography. It was underlined here and there, with slips of papers marking the spots.

Claudine's dressing table had been an amazing mass of perfumes, makeup, magazines, candies, but Meg's had only a Chinese vase (authentic . . . another thing Dad had probably sent) and a photo of her and some man. It was in color and looked as though it had been taken at a seashore. Recent it was, judging from the clothes. This, then, couldn't be the man who had figured in Aunt Meg's *tragic love affair*, as I'd once heard it called. I'd asked Jess to try to find out about it, and Ruthanne even, but none of us ever could.

I set down the photo, trying to remember exactly how it had been positioned, and opened the closet. Well, what a sight that was!

You could actually walk into that closet, it was so huge. Even Claudine, who flew to Paris periodically for the grand shopping, as she called it, couldn't match the number of garments hanging here.

On one overhead shelf I saw row after row of shoes, and handbags of every color and shape. The shelf on the other side had some hats . . . not many . . . and storage boxes labeled for each of the seasons. There were other boxes filled with photos and camera equipment.

The last box was pushed back a bit and had no label. It was sealed shut. I was holding it, trying to imagine what might be inside, when I heard a sound; it seemed to come from the back door. I absolutely froze, but then there was silence. Breathing a sigh of relief I scuttled to my room and closed the door.

Now, in daylight, I took stock of the room that was mine, at least for as long as I decided to stay. Not too bad, actually, considering that my taste had not been consulted.

I'd whisk off the floral bedspread however, as soon as my things arrived, and put on a madras cover. Instead of this dear little Renoir reproduction of two girls in a garden I'd tack up the poster of the Master, which I'd brought rolled up in my suitcase.

I flopped down on the chintz chair, wondering if I could find something in bamboo to replace it. Father had refused to let me ship my furniture. "You can replace it at any junk shop," he'd said. "The whole lot isn't worth freight charges."

Suddenly feeling tired again, I kicked off my shoes and lay on the bed. It seemed moments later that there was a tap at the door.

I almost said, "Go away," from force of habit, but then I realized my *ayah* wasn't here and that it was probably Aunt Meg. "Yes?" I rose up on my elbows.

Aunt Meg opened the door and peeked in. "Oh dear, I'm sorry. I didn't know."

"It's okay. What time is it?" And looked at my watch. "Six o'clock!"

"You've been out like a light for at least three hours. Do you feel up to showering and getting ready?"

What a nice hint that I hadn't bathed since arrival. "Oh, of course."

"We're due over at the McIntyres' in another hour. They're having a little welcome home dinner in your honor."

"Will Jess be there?"

"Of course. He said on the phone that he stopped by but no one seemed to be home. That reminds me. I'm having your own phone installed next week. If you want it."

"All right." Of course, she was just talking. It takes months to get a phone installed. "What shall I wear tonight?"

"It doesn't matter." She glanced at my bag, still unopened. "If you need anything, let me know. There are towels and things in the bathroom, of course."

Yes, yes, I get the message. I had heard from Claudine that Americans were really paranoid about being clean and that they used all kinds of things to get rid of any kind of body scent.

"I may need to have something pressed," I said. And then I remembered. There was no *ayah* to see that it got done. "Oh, well, I'll just shake something out."

Meg was looking at me in a way I couldn't fathom. To cover my uneasiness I babbled, "Indian gauze . . . cotton . . . doesn't need a great amount of ironing." I knelt, opened the largest bag and dragged out the lavender with its embroidery and ribbons. I held it up. "Is this suitable? It's not mussed much."

For just a few moments it was as though Meg didn't hear. Then her eyes went from me to the dress. "Lovely . . . lovely."

After she left I stared at my reflection in the mirror. I

hadn't broken out in hives or anything. So why that steady gaze of hers?

Oh, well. I went into the bath, turned on the water, and dropped my clothes. Perhaps Aunt Meg was simply staggered by my great beauty. And charm.

The loneliness that had slowly been creeping upon me during the day vanished the minute I again set eyes on Jess.

"Hey, Lindy! You look almost normal," he said, with just a shoulder hug this time. "Hey, Dad, doesn't she look great?"

"I'll say she does!" And Uncle Robert kissed me on each cheek and then the forehead and chin, the way he used to when I was a little girl. It was the kind of affection that always sent baby Ruthanne into a jealous fit. She'd tug at Uncle Robert and say, "*My* daddy! Go away, Linnie!" And then he'd put his arms around the two of us and say, "You're both my girls." But he'd have to kiss Ruthanne a couple of times to shut her up.

As we'd grown older the kissy stuff had stopped. Uncle Robert was still pleasant and loving but he didn't relate to older kids as well as he did to the little ones. My father, on the other hand, related better to older kids. He seemed not to care for babies at all, and I've sometimes wondered if that's why he and Claudine hadn't had any. (But there was also the possibility that he couldn't see Claudine raising a kid from scratch, since she'd done such a job of spoiling me, at least in Father's view.)

There was no cocktail hour as there'd been back in India. We sat down at table almost immediately, to food placed on the table all at once.

"Don't you just love roast beef?" Ruthanne asked after I'd taken a bite.

"Delicious." Actually, it tasted a bit flat to me.

"I think I'd starve rather than eat all that curried gook again. We have such a variety here. Wait until you've tasted some of the stuff."

"Don't listen," Jess advised, with a grin at his sister. "Ruthanne's taken a personal survey of every junk food outfit around here and finds it all wonderful."

"I do not! But some of it really is good. And so fast!"

"That's why they call them *fast-food chains*, ignorance," Jess said.

After dinner, Jess and I went with Ruthanne to her room. "This is a new first," Ruthanne said. "My getting out of clearing up and all. I've really become such a drudge. Maybe you'll get out of dishes, though, since Aunt Meg is so nice."

"I'm not looking for favors," I said.

Ruthanne gave a little sniff and flopped onto the bed. Jess and I sat on the floor, knees crossed.

"What's your reaction so far?" Jess asked. "To the States?"

I picked at a bit of shag carpeting. "I don't figure I've seen any of it yet. Except for the airport and the two houses."

"Oh, you'll love it, Lindsay," Ruthanne said. "I do."

"There's a lot to get used to at first," Jess said. "You may go into culture shock for a while."

"What things must I get used to?"

"The pace. The possibilities. What to eat, what to wear, where to go, who to hang out with."

"Hang out with?"

"Friends." He got up. "Look, I've got things to do. I'll see you later, Lindsay. Okay?"

"Sure." I waited until he left. "Did I say or do something wrong, Ruthanne?"

"No. Maybe it's just that you remind Jess of the hard time he had fitting in. Not that he wanted to all that much. Or even wants to now."

"Why do you say that?"

"It's true. Oh, he pretends. He wears U.S. clothes — but with some European touch. And when kids start goofing around he doesn't actually say anything but he doesn't join in either."

"Ruthanne, you can't expect Jess to change his personality just because others . . ."

"All right, then how about this? From all the possible choices what does Jess do but pick a Chinese girlfriend?"

"A *what?*"

"Chinese. American-Chinese, but foreign all the same."

"Jess has a *girlfriend?*"

Something in my tone caught Ruthanne off-guard. "I . . . well . . . I mean . . . hasn't he told you? Hasn't he written about Hope?"

"I guess I just forgot," I said. Faking a yawn, I got up. "I'm going to excuse myself and head back to the house," I said. "See if I can get into the new time pattern."

"You do look a bit wan and weary," Ruthanne said, unconsciously slipping into a British inflection. "I expect it's culture shock."

"I expect it is." She was half right. I'd had a bit of a shock.

Somehow, I'd never thought of Jess having a girlfriend. He never had before, in all those years. He'd always been there when I needed someone to confide in or ask for advice.

But now a *girlfriend*?

No matter. It wouldn't change things a bit. Jess would still be my pal as always. We'd been close too long for anyone else to come between us.

Chapter Four

On Sunday morning Aunt Meg and I were lounging around reading the papers when the phone rang. Carrying her coffee cup and still halfway reading the theater section, she walked out to the kitchen to answer. "Oh, Lindsay, it's for you," she called out. And as I passed her, "Jess."

"What are you doing?" he asked.

"Reading the comics. I *have* read the news."

"Look, the reason I'm calling is, I wondered if you wanted to go over to the *indoors* and play some tennis?"

"Now? I haven't my racket."

"No problem. We can fix you up. Hope's family could open a store."

"Quite." I paused. "Who is Hope?" I pretended I'd never heard of her.

"She's a girl I know. Top-drawer player. Puts me to shame. She comes from a family of tennis freaks."

"Well, Jess, perhaps some other time."

Pause. "Okay, if you change your mind let me know."

Actually, I'd expected him to coax a bit. Back in the living room I was feeling decidedly let down when the phone rang again. He *was* going to plead, then. Or better yet, he'd broken the tennis date and was coming over to lend cheer and that sort of thing. "Hi again," I said, picking up the phone. "I rather knew you'd call back. Persistent little runt, aren't you?"

There was a pause, and then a hesitant, "Meg?"

I wanted to die. "Actually, it's not. I'll just fetch her."

"It's for you," I said, going back, red-faced. "A man."

Meg took off the reading glasses that made her look older. "Thanks," she said, and left.

I strained to hear, but there were only murmurings. I snatched up the comics just before she came back.

"That was Eliot," she said. "You'll meet him one of these days. He knows all about you, of course."

Of course. "If you want to go out with him don't hesitate on my account," I said. "I have plans." Or could have.

"Oh? I thought you might like to go clothes shopping. The mall stores are open on Sunday."

"I have enough clothes." My snappish answer seemed to prick her like needles. "And anyway . . . (what could I say to soothe her?) I think I should wait. To see what the other girls are wearing."

"Good idea. What are your plans for today?"

I needn't tell you, you know. "Jess has invited me to play tennis."

"Oh, wonderful. That will get you into the swing of things."

If she meant that as a play on words, I didn't smile. "I expect it will take a while to get my game up." A very long while. Like twenty years. "I'm a bit rusty, you know. Oh, and don't plan on my being here for dinner. Jess and I are going to one of those quick-food places." What I'd do would be to wait until the game was over and the girl gone and then invite Jess to dine with me. Money was no problem. I had quite a lot.

Afraid that Aunt Meg might overhear my explanations, I headed straightaway for Jess's house and told him I'd had a change of heart. He didn't seem particularly surprised.

"We've got a while," he said "so how about my driving you around to show off the suburb? It's pretty nice in places, although this isn't the greatest weather. Still too cold, even though we're ending up spring vacation. I'll show you the school. It's within walking distance for us."

The school, as we parked in front of it, looked to me like an airplane hangar or a warehouse. "It's so huge," I said.

"The enrollment's over two thousand."

"Two thousand!"

"Yeh, you won't even know some of the kids. Not like the old American School."

"Are they all spilling over with energy and all that?" I remembered the thundering herd coming aboard the plane.

"Some, not all. Just be careful when classes change. They come charging down the hall like bullocks."

Exactly. Oh dear. "Is there a lot of . . . changing classes?" We'd done so only for science back in the old school.

"All the time. Your life's governed by bells." He glanced at me and must have seen the cold, raw fear on my face. "Hey, don't worry. You'll get into the swing soon."

Was everything here gotten into by a swing?

"I rather imagine," I said, "school can be put off for a while. I can just wait until the proper mood occurs."

"You don't want to do that," he said, shifting the stick into drive. "Besides, you're already registered for tomorrow."

"I am?"

"Aunt Meg was over, getting it all set up a couple of weeks ago. They're expecting you."

How nice, I thought. How nice to have it all arranged without any consultation with me. It was only my life.

"She's really nice, isn't she? Aunt Meg?" Jess waited for a red light to change. "I expected her to be . . . it's hard to remember now . . . but kind of stiff and formal. Instead, she's . . ." We drove on.

"She's what?"

"Well, you know. Warm, friendly. Lots of fun when you get to know her. I should have realized she'd have a lot on the ball, considering her job and all."

"That positively awes Ruthanne."

"Oh, well. Ruthanne. See, there's the sports center up ahead. That brick building on the left."

"It looks a bit grim."

"Wait until you see inside. Besides the courts they have exercise rooms, a swimming pool, a sauna, a whirlpool. . . ."

"Jess, I hope you don't expect me to play today. I just came along to watch."

"Okay. If you change your mind, though, Hope's bringing along an extra racket."

I still didn't have tennis shorts or shoes, though, and I was awfully glad I didn't when I saw what a crack tennis player Hope was. She was better than any woman I'd watched over at the British courts. Better than anyone else in this center, in fact. Even Rajee would have been hard put to beat her.

Her greeting had been, to my great surprise, easy and accepting. I could have been anyone . . . and not the dear longtime friend of Jess that I really was.

Sitting on the sidelines, I marveled at the girl's good

nature. She laughed a lot . . . and Jess laughed too . . .
mostly at his errors. "I'm so blasted clumsy!" he said at
one point.

"Don't worry," Hope called out. "It was a tough return!"

So she was tactful as well as proficient. Attractive, too,
in an unexpected way. Instead of the fragile lotus flower
I'd somehow expected Hope was fairly tall and solidly
built. Also (and this I could hardly forgive her) she had a
perfect tan, even at this time of year.

I looked at my own pale, freckled arm in disgust. But
Jess, out there, looked just as washed out. Besides our
light, freckled skin, we also had strawberry blond hair in
common. I, in fact, looked more like Jess's sister than did
Ruthanne.

When Jess came out after showering I told him I was
taking him to dinner so I could experience quick food.

"*Fast* food," he corrected with a smile.

"Whatever difference does it make?"

"It makes people look at you. That's the difference. Ah,
here's Hope." We walked outside. "Hey, Whiz, want to go
out for tacos or something?"

"I'd love to, but we have relatives coming over and besides I have that paper to finish."

Before Jess could coax I said, "Some other time, then?
Nice meeting you, Hope."

"Same here. See you at school, probably." She took off
in a little yellow car that had Trans Am painted on its side.

Jeff watched her go. "Neat little number, that."

"The girl or the car?"

He laughed. "Both. I think I'll get a compact car myself, when I save up enough money."

"You mean . . . kids have their own cars here?"

"Sure. There's no public transportation except for a few special busses to malls, airports, and so on. There are no such things as chauffeurs, either . . . unless you count parents. All kids sixteen or over drive. In fact, that's how I met Hope."

We got into his car and pulled out of the lot. "I was working at the car wash one Saturday last fall and she brought in her Trans Am. I noticed her but didn't have the courage to say much. Then a little while later she brought in a Buick and after that a Corvair. So I asked her if she was triplets and she said no, she was just stuck doing this family thing."

"Three cars! How extravagant."

"Not really. Her family just goes off in all directions at once. What did you think of Hope?"

"Crack tennis player."

"I mean personally."

"Jess, we hardly exchanged three sentences."

"Too bad she couldn't join us. But you'll have plenty of time to get acquainted."

"I expect I'll make my own friends. Tell me, what kind of food will it be? What *fast* food?"

"Your choice. See, up ahead? Burger King, McDonald's, or we could get roast beef, tacos, pizza, seafood, gyros. . . ." We were on the highway now. "Oh, well, let's start with hamburgers."

It was truly amazing. We went inside, found a booth, Jess walked to the counter and within minutes we had hamburgers. Also French fries and Cokes. "In a way," I said, "this reminds me of Paris."

"Paris?"

"Don't you remember? On the Champs-Elysées, the Mc-

Donald's inside that building? Your own father took us there."

"I'd forgotten about that."

I looked at him, wondering what else he had forgotten. Our seeing the Taj Mahal together, at dawn? The afternoon we spent meditating and experiencing the peace and holiness of the Birla Temple in Delhi? The scores of things we used to do and discuss? I reached for the Coke. "Jess, do you ever dream you're back in India?"

"I used to, but not so much anymore. See, Lindsay, everything's so different here. It seems hyper and even . . . well, a little phony at first. But then you get into it and you see it's the way to be. To get things done."

"What things, Jess?"

"Oh . . . you know. Everything. It's hard to explain, but you'll see what I mean after you're here for a while."

"I probably won't be here all that long. I have a commitment, you know."

"What kind of commitment?"

I put my left hand forward. "See this ring?"

"Where did you get it?"

"From Rajee. You know what that means."

"I can't say I do. He gives you a star sapphire . . ."

"It's a symbol, Jess. Of our undying devotion."

Jess studied my face. "You're not seriously thinking of marrying Rajee, are you? You couldn't be."

"And why not?"

"Because . . ."

"Because he's Indian?"

"No, of course not. But . . . well . . . your age. You're only seventeen."

"I shan't be forever, now shall I? Anyway, Jess, I'd just as soon not discuss it anymore."

I could actually feel him thinking, who brought up the subject? But all he said was, "What do you want to talk about?"

"Oh . . . school. You might tell me what to expect, so long as it's all been settled. First, what shall I wear? I don't want to stand out in the crowd, you know."

"All right. Scratch the sari."

"Really, Jess, do you take me for a blathering idiot?"

"Wear a skirt with a sweater or blouse. Now, the way the school's run is this . . ." And he went on to describe the layout. Then he outlined the rules, and told me about lockers, class bells, tardy slips, detention, special help, counselors, and so on until I was mentally exhausted. "Please, I can't absorb any more," I said. "I'll never get it all sorted out."

"Sure you will. Just follow the crowd. And don't panic."

"Panic? Why should I panic? You make it sound like such fun . . . like being in a penitentiary. What time do I enter?"

"Just before eight. I'll pick you up at seven-thirty."

It was then the cold realization hit me. I'd be absolutely on my own once Jess and I reached the school. A stranger in a strange land . . . just like the book I'd read. Only worse.

Later, letting me in, Aunt Meg said brightly, "Hi, there. Have a nice time?"

"Yes, rather."

"Want to join me for a while? There's a good show just starting on TV."

"Thank you, but I have letters to write." Basic politeness prevented my just walking away. Casually, I said, "I understand from Jess that I'm to start school tomorrow."

Meg put a hand to her throat and colored. "You mean to say I didn't tell you? Oh, Lindsay, I *am* sorry! But look, if you want to wait, to get settled in first . . ."

Playing the martyr, I sighed. "I may as well start tomorrow and be done with it."

"Look, Lindsay, I . . . I'm new at this . . . being a . . . having a young person around. If I goof, please tell me. It isn't intentional. I want us to be . . ."

"Yes. Well, thank you." I turned to leave.

"Listen, if you're hungry . . . I mean any time . . . for heaven's sakes, help yourself. And if there's anything I can get . . . some food you prefer . . ."

"That's very kind, I'm sure."

"Uh . . . well. Good night, then."

"Good night." I got ready for bed . . . actually I did wear pajamas . . . and started another letter to Rajee. The first, which I'd written that morning, had been full of love and lament. Since I didn't choose to go in that direction again, I began one full of cynicism.

> *Ruthanne is as tiresome as ever, now showing off how very American she has become. For example, "It's a real drag, not having my own bath." (Jess tells me Ruthanne showers and shampoos every single morning. She blow-dries her hair — that's hard to explain — and makes herself up like a film star. I wonder Aunt Janice permits it.) Jess is as sweet and comforting as usual, though he has a girlfriend now. Hope, the girlfriend, finds everything amusing. I expect Jess will tire of her soon.*

I could feel my stomach rumbling, desiring a bit more than hamburger and Coke. Milk. Milk would be just the thing.

I eased my bedroom door open. No sound from the TV. Good. Most likely Aunt Meg had decided to go off to bed.

I went to the kitchen and had just poured the milk when Meg came in with a cup and saucer. Startled, I mumbled, "I . . . uh . . . since you said . . ."

"Of course." She pulled out a box from the cupboard. "Here are some cookies. I hope you'll like them."

"Thank you. They look awfully good, actually."

"Well . . . again, good night. See you in the morning."

Odd. She looked as though she'd been crying. Missed her boyfriend, I expect. Must have been sheer torture for her, getting through the weekend without him. I went back to my room, taking the milk and cookies, and continued the letter to Rajee.

> As for Aunt Meg, I wrote, she's all right so far. Hasn't tried to boss me about, but I expect she will in time. Try to, I mean.

I really wasn't in the mood to write, but I did want to get off another letter, to keep them flowing, as promised.

> Rajee, please forgive this boring recitation. I'm worried, rather, about starting school tomorrow. Things here are all so strange. I'll write again, once they've begun to sort out.
>
> Your ever-loving
> Lindsay

Aunt Meg had given me overseas stamps and said she'd mail my letters downtown, where service was speedier. I propped this one on the kitchen table alongside the one I'd written earlier. Even though Aunt Meg was undoubtedly part of the anti-Rajee conspiracy I knew somehow I could trust her to send my letters off.

At the moment my chief concern was about tomorrow. Just thinking of it made a cold, hard knot form in the pit of my stomach. Would it be dreadful? I rather imagined it would. *Don't panic*, Jess had said.

What a comfort he was. Never mind about tomorrow. I was as scared as I could get right now.

Chapter Five

True to his word, Jess escorted me to the school. Even though he'd told me about kids driving I just couldn't believe the number of cars parked side by side in the lot, so close you could have walked on the roofs. "Do you mean to say, even with school buses this many students drive?"

"Yeh. It's like a disgrace or something, to ride the bus after you have a license."

"Incredible."

Inside, Jess took me down the hall to the principal's office. The dean was supposed to "orient" me, as he put it, but there were all kinds of interruptions. It was after eleven when he finally handed over my schedule, my locker number, and the school handbook. "Lindsay, why don't you go to lunch now? Then you can check out the place before your afternoon classes."

I wasn't overly fond of his casual dismissal of me nor the way he'd called me *Lindsay* instead of *Miss Collins*, but I went off agreeably enough.

Out in the hall, I knew I needed to use the ladies' but hadn't a clue where it might be. A fairly pleasant-looking girl was coming down the hall and I asked her where the W.C. was.

"The *what?*"

"The loo? The toilet?"

"Oh. Right around the corner." She gave me a faintly disapproving look and walked on.

At least I can find the cafeteria, I thought, when I came out into the hall again. Following the scent of warm food, I pushed into a room where women were working. Mistake. It wasn't the dining area but the kitchen itself.

"You're not allowed in here, miss," one monstrous woman stated in none-too-charming a tone.

"Sorry, I'm sure. I only happen to be looking for the cafeteria."

"Won't find it here," she said. "It's two doors down." She said something in an undertone to the woman next to her and they both laughed.

The door to the cafeteria was standing open . . . double doors, actually, and so far there were just a few students sitting at tables or going down a line where food was heaped in steaming containers. There was a variety of things I couldn't identify and all sorts of machines with handles, and glasses and cups and things in packets sitting about. I might have turned and fled if a woman, bringing out a stack of trays, hadn't handed me one. I got in line.

"Yes, miss," a woman said, brandishing a huge ladle, "what'll it be? Soup or chili?"

"Uh . . . what sort of soup is it?"

"Clam chowder."

"I see. Well, actually, I'm not sure I care about either."

"Suit yourself." And she turned to the next kid in line.

"Would you move?" he muttered.

I did, taking anything offered. I'd suddenly lost my appetite.

At one big machine I stalled, wondering what the spigots were for and how one managed them. Someone reached in front of me to snatch up a small carton of milk

(I knew, because it said MILK). I took the same and just as I turned a girl jostled me, almost upsetting my tray.

"Well, really," I said without thinking, "can't you look where you're going?"

The girl gave me a look. "No, I *cahn't*," she said, imitating my accent. She and the other two girls laughed and moved away.

The woman at the cashier's desk looked at my loaded tray and then at me, but shrugged when I showed her the lunch pass. "Okay."

I went to a vacant table in the farthest corner, where I sat just mooshing the food around on the plate. I also made a shamble of the milk carton, which seemed sealed for all eternity.

I was about to give up when Jess appeared. "Hey! Looks like you made it just fine!"

I shrugged and tears nearly came to my eyes, but Jess didn't notice, occupied as he was in forking down the food.

"The chow's always best at the beginning of the week before they have leftovers to disguise in cute little ways," he said. "So how's it going so far? What classes . . . ?"

He paused as a hand ruffled his hair, and we both looked up. "Hey, Rita," he said, "how are you? Good spring break? And Cindy and Laura . . ."

"Lori," the girl said. The same girl who'd jostled me back there in line. "When are you going to remember it's *Lori*?"

"At least I remember *you*," he said. Hearing his tone, I felt I might get sick. "Oh, hey, Rita, Cindy, and *Lori* . . . see, I'm a quick learner . . . this is Lindsay."

"Hi," the Lori creature said. "Hey, it's great to meet you!" The two girls behind Jess, whom he couldn't see, gave simpering little smiles.

Jess, the insufferable beast, motioned for the girls to join us. "Lindsay just got here from India," he explained.

"India! Oh, wow! That's like really exotic. Were you born there or what?"

"I just lived there for a while. As did Jess."

"Hey!" Lori piped. "No kidding. Hey, Jess, you'll have to tell me all about it some time."

I couldn't take any more. With a curt, "See you later, Jess," I hitched the strap of my bag onto my shoulder and started out. A woman wearing a white uniform stopped me.

"Just where do you think you're going, miss?"

I stared at her. "I can't" (it came out *cahn't*, of course) "see that that's any concern of yours!"

"Well, it *is* my concern, the trays. You don't just walk out and leave them like that. The idea!"

Feeling my face flame, I stomped back and picked up the tray. Jess and the girls looked up. "All right, what do you wish me to do with it?" I said to the woman. "Of course, I know what I should *like* to do with it."

"Just over there," she said, motioning, "with the others. And watch what you say, young lady, or I'll put out a report on you."

Jess rushed out after me and stopped me in the hall by grabbing my arms. "Hey, I'm sorry. I should have . . ."

I shrugged out of his grasp. "Just leave me alone, will you? Go back to . . . whatever her name is. And do pick up your tray. I wouldn't want *you* to be yelled at and embarrassed beyond belief."

"Lindsay, it happens all the time here. Kids try to sneak out . . ."

"Oh, bravo. Well put."

"Listen, like you, I thought servants did the picking up

45

when I first came. That's what we were used to. But here people look after themselves."

He'd taken hold of one arm again. "Then let go of me," I said. "So I can get about the business of looking after myself."

That evening Jess repeated his apologies.

"It's all right," I said. I had to forgive him. There was no one else in whom I could confide. "I don't mind, really, except for those girls."

"Fleabrains," Jess said. "Nobodies."

"You were certainly chatting them up."

"Doesn't mean a thing. Just a way of getting along."

I longed to point out to Jess that he had never played the insincere role before but it wouldn't do, right after we'd made a truce. "I feel more in a foreign land here than at any time overseas," I told him. "Why is that, I wonder?"

"You're tuned into *British* English, that's all. *American* English has key words you just have to pick up gradually."

"Like what?"

"Uh . . . like this. 'We're trading in our Cougar for a Rabbit.'"

"Jess, that doesn't make one bit of sense."

"Sure it does. Those are types of cars. Now, suppose I said, 'hang a left'?"

"Could it mean *put a leftist to death?*"

"Good try. It means *turn left at the corner.* What's an idiot box? Give up? The TV."

"You mean *telly.* Oh, Jess, I'll never catch on, I know."

"Sure you will. Get a little notebook and write things down. That's what I did at first."

We heard the car and then Aunt Meg came in. "Oh, Jess what a relief," she said. "You let Lindsay in. It wasn't until I was halfway home that I remembered I hadn't given her a key of her own, or even told her about your family having one."

"No problem," Jess said.

"Lindsay," Meg said, "I'm so sorry. What a way to treat you!"

"It's okay."

"Look, don't be polite. If I mess up on things, let me know. My mind gets so scrambled with details I sometimes don't know where I'm at. You're probably starving."

"No." But the minute she said it my stomach started rumbling.

"I'll just get rid of the briefcase and out of these heels and will be right with you. I want to hear all about your day." She smiled and left.

Jess glanced at his watch. "Got to leave."

"Okeydokey." That was a phrase we'd picked up from an old film and which we used at every opportunity. Only now it seemed to glide right past Jess.

"I forgot to mention . . . I have to be at school early tomorrow for practice," he said. "Should I ask Ruthanne to stop by for you?"

Abandoned already. "Oh, no, I'll be fine."

"Okay, see you at noon in the cafeteria. From now on we'll be there at the same time."

I shrugged. Hungry though I was at the moment from having had no lunch, I couldn't see myself entering that hall of horror ever again.

Chapter Six

It was truly astonishing. Within forty minutes Meg and I were sitting down to eat. I believed even I could learn to cook if all I had to do was stick chops under a broiler, toss bags of vegetables into boiling water and simply rinse off other vegetables before cutting them up for salad. I still couldn't get used to drinking water from the tap without boiling it first, and using ice cubes made from that same water.

"Lindsay," Aunt Meg said, as I was tucking into the salad, "can you think of anything else, other than the key, that I've forgotten? Oh, I know one thing . . . a list of telephone numbers. The McIntyres' is one and I can give you the number of a woman across the street who's usually home. And then, of course, my office number and the one for when we're on mike."

"On *what?*"

"Microphone. We're on the air from one until three but I can still take calls during commercials. Or else you can leave a message and I'll get back to you."

"What do you do . . . on mike?"

"It's a news, helpful hints, and interview show. Maybe you can catch it on a day when there's no school. Some time I'll take you to the studio with me, if you'd like. There's not much to see, actually, but there could be some celebrity you'd like to meet." She frowned. "But you probably haven't heard of most of these people. Strange."

"Strange?"

"To think what a totally different life you've led. Lindsay, I'm really dying to hear details of it. Your . . . father tells me some . . ."

"Father? When did you last see him?"

"Gee, it was . . . it's hard to remember."

She was fibbing, I could tell. Most people couldn't tell when I did it. Except for Jess. "Father was in the States in January. Did you see him then?"

"Yes, that's when it was, I guess. Is there anything else I could get for you? How about some ice cream?"

"Yes, all right. Thank you."

She put our dinner and salad plates into the sink, opened the freezer side of the fridge and pulled out a container. "Strawberry okay? Or Neopolitan?"

"Either one." Why was she flustered? Was it because I wasn't supposed to know about the little conference with her brother? Was that when they'd laid plans to get me over here? It was to my advantage that Aunt Meg wasn't a parent, used to hiding things from kids. She'd be easier to manipulate than Claudine, who sometimes clammed up on orders from Father.

As I sat there watching Aunt Meg pour boiling water over a tea bag I thought, she probably knows all the gory details about the time they . . . Claudine and Father . . . came home to find Rajee and me in the house alone. An enormous fuss over nothing, that was. I took the ice cream and cup of tea. "Aren't you having any?"

"No, I'm trying to cut down on calories and also caffeine. Are you sure this won't keep you awake?"

"Positive. I drink it all the time at home." That's what Rajee and I were doing that day . . . drinking tea. I'd brewed it myself since all the house servants were out at the time. I had to smile now, remembering how Rajee had stood there literally shaking when Father dressed him down. He'd fully expected, he told me later, to have officers come to his home later and arrest him. Honestly!

Father, though quick to anger, didn't hold on to it long. Whether or not he actually believed the innocence of it all, he never mentioned the incident again. I assumed he'd forgotten about it. But because of all that here I was now, living with an aunt who was a stranger to me. It would be interesting to see what kind of person she really was, once we got past the politeness stage.

On the first full day of school I managed to find my way around because a secretary in the office gave me a map of the school with my rooms circled and numbered in sequence.

She'd also given me an armload of books and shown me my locker. This Tuesday morning, though, I thought I'd play it safe by carrying all the books about with me. I wasn't sure I could get to my locker between classes without being late, and Jess had warned me against that deadly sin. "They throw you to the crocodiles," he said. "Actually, they toss you into after-school detention with a beastly teacher, so it amounts to the same."

Most of the teachers I happened to have were cordial, if not absolutely charmed to have an extra set of papers to grade at this late date. Some classes, like world history and English literature, were bound to be a breeze, but I was totally muddled by math and chemistry.

"Don't let it get to you," Jess said at lunch. Raw hunger had steered me to the cafeteria again, but this time Jess was there to run interference, as he put it. We sat in an out-of-the-way area. "They have tutors if you need them. I had one for calculus. Or you could go to summer school to catch up." He demonstrated the easy way to open a milk carton. "How were your teachers this morning?"

"Okay. The one teaching German . . ."

"Mr. Mitchell?"

"That's the one . . . asked me to join the Language Club. What's it all about?"

"It's just a bunch of kids who get into different cultures."

"Get into? In what way?"

"They show slides or movies of countries and go to ethnic restaurants."

"That sounds rather a bore. Why don't they simply go to the country itself and find out about it first hand?"

Jess frowned. "Lindsay, don't talk like that. Kids can't handle it."

"Whatever do you mean?"

"It sounds so snobbish."

"Well! Thank you very much!"

"I'm only telling you. It's best to play down all the places you've lived and things you've seen. Cool it for a while."

"Jess, I'd be ever so much obliged if you'd speak basic English." As his face reddened slightly I added, "Sorry, I'm sure, but since you're the only person who understands what I'm going through . . ."

"I know." He hunched his shoulders slightly. "I guess I'm a little touchy because you remind me of some of my worst moments. I'm still not sure of myself."

"Oh, Jess, how did we ever get into this muddle? What cruel fate was it that sent us here?"

"I want to be here."

"You do?"

"Yes, and so will you after a while."

"But then your whole family's here. It's different for you. I've been dumped on these shores because I'm an embarrassment."

"What?"

"Oh, don't play the innocent. Surely you've heard about Rajee and me."

"Heard what?"

He honestly seemed not to know. If Jess could catch me out in a fib I most certainly could catch him. "The day we were at the bungalow together. Oh, it was all perfectly innocent. It was just bad luck that there was no one about to back up our story."

"And you're saying that's why . . . Oh, Lindsay, come on."

"Come on yourself. You know very well that if Father had insisted, Rajee would have been made to marry me, since I'd been compromised. It's the custom over there."

"Well, it's not here. You'll flip . . . you'll be amazed . . . over what goes on. Anyway, I just can't believe your father and Claudine would be so shook up . . . so outraged . . . that they'd ship you over here because of that. It's got to be something else."

"There *is* nothing else. No reason at all. Is there?"

Jess looked thoughtful. "Maybe they thought that, being an American, you ought to have a shot at living here. While you're still young."

I took out my notebook. "I'd better record some of these strange sayings. *Shot at* . . . meaning chance?" I wrote it down and added *cool it, you'll flip, and shook up* along with their meanings.

"What else do you have there?" Jess asked.

"*Squared away, cornball attitude, never mind the snow job, not playing with a full deck.*"

"That should see you through any evening in a drawing room," Jess said. "What are you doing tonight?"

"Studying, I expect."

"If it'll help, I'll come over and study with you. Just to help out at first."

"That's awf'ly nice of you, Jess."

"There's one condition, though. Aunt Meg has to be there."

"Why do you say that?"

He picked up his tray. "There aren't any servants about. So *she* had better be around. If you get disgraced again, wherever could they send you?" He laughed and walked away.

I gave a little laugh, too, and followed him, after first depositing my tray properly. But after we'd separated in the hall I stood there for a moment wondering. If I hadn't been sent here because of Rajee, then *why*? So I could learn to be the true American girl, as Jess had suggested? If that were so, why the rush? Surely it could have waited until this school term ended.

There was something more to it, I was sure. But what that something was, only three people knew. Father — who would have made an excellent espionage agent, lips sealed and all. Claudine, who was no doubt under orders to stay silent. And Meg, a working member of the conspiracy gang. Oh yes, add to that Aunt Janice and Uncle Robert, but they'd never tell.

It wasn't fair. My life was one giant puzzle, but with no

clue as to the missing pieces. How was I to put it all to-gether?

All I could do was wait, and listen, and keep alert. Someone, sometime would make a slip. I rather thought it might be Aunt Meg.

Chapter Seven

I decided to go to the Language Club meeting after school on Friday because they were going to show color slides of Hong Kong. I rather fancied seeing again some of the spots where I'd had spectacular adventures with Jess.

Before showing the slides, there was a business meeting. Then the program chairman, a Lily someone, announced what she called a preshow learning experience. I blinked in disbelief when she brought out a bowl of rice and a pair of chopsticks. "Would anyone care to *try* before I demonstrate the correct method of using these?" she asked with a smirky smile.

No one budged. Jess refused to return my look.

"Alan?"

"Not me."

Lily smiled. "Hope?"

Hope gave her throaty laugh. "Don't look at me. I never could get the hang of those things." The kids laughed.

I couldn't let this go on. "I'll do it," I said, getting up.

The group looked at me in a not particularly kindly fashion as I went forward.

"What's your name again?" Lily asked.

"Lindsay." I took the chopsticks, placed them properly, and picked up the rice without dropping so much as a grain. "Here." I handed back the chopsticks and bowl.

Lily cleared her throat. "That's one way. So guys, the next time you're in a Chinese restaurant, use chopsticks."

We saw the slides with recorded comment. After the meeting Hope drove Jess and me home. "What did you think of the group?" she asked me.

"Is this a case where I should be polite or candid?"

Hope laughed. "Let's hear it."

"Very well. I can't see why students who pretend such great and genuine interest in foreign places would oh and ah in wonder over slides obviously taken by a travel agency not the least bit interested in showing the underbellies of nations."

"Whoooh!" Hope laughed. "I asked for that."

"To get down to specifics," I went on, "those photographs of the water people didn't half show the squalor of their lives."

"You mentioned that during the showing," Jess said.

"As well I might. I was only trying to inject a bit of realism into what looked like perpetual holiday life for all."

"Kids don't want realism," Jess said, "in things like that."

"Well, hard cheese to them. They should wake up and see how some people actually struggle just to exist."

"And how are they supposed to do that?"

"By being more open to people who really know."

"Come on," Jess said. "They're trying to understand."

"Oh, really? I got the distinct impression that they feel it perfectly proper to discuss a place provided one's never actually been there."

"She has a point, Jess," Hope said. "The group does take a kind of technicolor tourist attitude toward those places. You two really should lay it on the line . . . what it's like away from the tour groups."

I took out my notebook. "What does *lay it on the line* mean?"

Hope laughed. "Cut out the baloney."

"Tell it like it is," Jess said.

"Really! You're making it so muddled I don't know what to write."

"You know what, Lindsay?" Hope said, turning down our street. "I think you should just take it easy and go with the flow. Relax and let the words sink in."

"Or I'll sink in the process."

"Nonsense. Jess caught on, didn't you, Jess?"

We'd reached Aunt Meg's house, which saved him from admitting that he, too, had kept a notebook. "Thanks for the lift," I said, pleased to remember that *lift* here meant a ride and not an elevator.

"You're welcome," Hope said. "And Lindsay, let me know when and if you still want to go clothes shopping. I adore helping others spend money. Don't I, Jess?"

"You bet. I'm still paying off some of that Christmas shopping."

As I went into the house I couldn't help but wonder if it had been Hope's idea, then, to buy me the butterfly cloisonné necklace last holiday. I didn't like thinking it might have been.

Meg was home. I thought it a bit odd, the way she hovered in the hall, but when I got to my room I saw why. A telephone! My own telephone there by the bed!

"I thought you'd be pleased," Aunt Meg said, standing in the doorway, with a kind of cute grin on her face.

"It's incredible. Do you have some sort of government connection?"

"Nope. Just routine commercialism."

"But does it actually work?" I picked up the receiver. "Yes, there's the tone."

"It's a separate line," she said. "So you can have privacy in your calls and I . . ."

And you can talk to your boy friend, Eliot, who knows all about me.

". . . I can rattle on with business calls when I need to."

"Can I call anyplace?" (Like India, I thought. Wouldn't Rajee be surprised!)

"Anyplace in the world. Ummm. Within reason."

"Oh. Does that mean I'm not to call . . . my father, for instance?"

"Well, surely that isn't necessary?"

"I'll pay, of course. I have money." I kicked off my shoes. "Mail takes ages. I know I haven't been here long, but I have the feeling that something is going on over there. Something I don't know about."

Aunt Meg had already taken off the gray striped jacket of her suit and now she fingered the buttons of the ruffled blouse. "I . . . uh . . . suppose you might as well know."

Pause. "Know . . . what?"

"Daniel and Claudine haven't been getting along too well."

Relief. "Is that all. They bicker all the time."

"This seems to be beyond bickering."

"Beyond . . . what do you mean exactly?"

"They've decided on a trial separation."

"What? But why?"

Aunt Meg swept back the forward-swinging hair. "Apparently they want to get more perspective on their problem. It's been difficult for Claudine, being in a foreign country, away from family and friends. And expected to jump right into the role of American wife and mother."

"Well, if Father expected Claudine to play the heavy parent with me he was all wrong. She wasn't the type."

"Lindsay, I really don't know the details. All I know is that she's back in Paris. Time will tell if they get back together or . . ." She brushed back her hair again. "I'd better change and get dinner started." She left.

I flung myself onto the bed. *Separated!* Well, that was something of a shock. I knew they argued a lot. Father often got annoyed at Claudine's careless ways and his somewhat stuffy attitudes drove her crazy. But separated? Why now?

There was something that had become worse, and that was Claudine's drinking. Father ignored it for a while. After all, he drank too, but moderately. He first took a stand the one time I was involved. It wasn't any major event. Father, in fact, wouldn't even have known about it if that reprehensible Shafi, chauffeur and stool pigeon, hadn't informed him. I could just see Shafi wringing his skinny hands and whimpering, "Oh, Sahib, it much distresses me to relate the wrongdoing in your absence."

Claudine and I could have kept it from Father, the knowledge that our car side-swiped a cart of vegetables being drawn by bullock to early morning market. The beast wasn't even touched and Claudine more than paid for the ruined vegetables. But Shafi had spotted the smudges of squashed produce along the length of the car. And worse luck, the farmer turned out to be a distant relative of his.

"And what," Father asked Claudine later, "were you doing, driving about at that hour?"

Claudine pouted. "Cherie, it was nothing. Just a little drive to clear the heads."

"To clear your heads? Of what?"

Claudine realized she'd blundered. Shafi hadn't known *that*.

"Well?" Father was glowering now. At Claudine's silence he turned to me. "Lindsay? You know, and you'd better tell me."

Claudine clasped her hands. "It was not the idea of Lindsay, Daniel. It was mine." She swallowed. "I thought it time to teach her how a lady should drink the champagne. *C'est necessaire, n'est-ce pas?*" Claudine always lapsed into French when she was under stress. "So we open the bottle and I teach her . . . like so . . ." She daintily lifted an imaginary glass.

"A bottle?"

Claudine tried for an innocent girlish air. "Cherie, it was a long evening, and I was so desolate that you were gone so long away . . . and so was Lindsay, *pauvre petite*."

"Never mind the *pauvre petite*. I'll deal with her later. Now, Claudine, I want it clearly understood that when I am away . . . on business . . . so that you can live in the lap of luxury and not have to . . ."

"Oooo . . . so angry. Tsk. You break my heart."

Father looked as though he could, in fact, cheerfully wring her neck, but then Claudine's tears began to flow, quietly, like a cherub's, and Father sent me from the room.

There was more shouting on Father's part. I hung around listening for a while, along with my *ayah*, who showed a vast interest in such things. The shouting and Claudine's sobs finally quieted and after a bit there was silence. I drifted away. Some time later, after I'd already eaten, she and Father asked that trays be sent in, and I didn't see the two of them for the rest of the night. Father never did deal with me. Or maybe he had. He'd sent me away, hadn't he? Was it because of Claudine not being a fit parent, and not my friendship with Rajee? Or was it a combination of both?

I felt fairly certain of one thing — they'd planned the separation before I was sent away, but didn't see fit to tell me.

I felt a bit guilty when I went to the kitchen and saw the table already set and things almost cooked.

"Is there something I could do?" I asked a bit lamely.

Meg gave me a quick glance. "If you want to take out the rolls . . ." She handed me a basket.

"You baked?"

Meg laughed. "Only heated. Some day when I really have time . . . a big bunch of time . . . I'm going to make them from scratch."

"Why bother if you can do it the easy way?"

"But it's not the same." She finished putting the food onto the table and we sat down. "Surely you know that, though. I'll bet Claudine was a super cook."

"Claudine? Not a bit. She couldn't so much as boil a turnip."

"But . . . but she's French."

A pause, and then we both laughed.

"Stupid, my saying that. But you just assume that all French girls . . ."

"Claudine isn't quite the typical French girl. Besides, she was raised in a convent, you know, and claims she was never let near the kitchen. I don't believe that a bit. She's just lazy." I buttered a roll. "Fun, though."

Aunt Meg was quiet. Then, "You miss her, don't you?"

"Yes, now and then." I mooshed the mashed potatoes

with my fork. "I'm wondering if I'll ever see her again." My voice broke slightly.

"Oh, Lindsay, of course you will! Even if they get . . . even if it doesn't work out any longer, the marriage, there's no reason why . . ."

The telephone rang. I got up and answered. "It's for you," I said. "Some man."

"Oh. It must be Eliot. I'll take it in the other room. Hang up when I answer, will you, Lin?"

"Sure." In a few moments she said a rather tentative "Hello," and he said, "It's me, Luv. How . . ."

I hung up. It seemed to be my fate always to be shut out when grownups had something to say to each other.

In my room a bit later I sat cross-legged on the bed and started to read the assigned chapters of *The Scarlet Letter*. But instead, my mind kept going back to Father and Claudine. *Separated.* What a cold word. And then I let myself remember the words I'd heard that particular night some weeks ago and had tried to put out of my mind.

It was quite late. I'd been asleep for at least a little while when I awakened to the sound of their angry voices, coming from the verandah.

Claudine, I knew, had been drinking all afternoon and was probably still at it. She must have been pacing because suddenly her voice came to me clearly: "Oh, that's a wonderful idea. Marvelous. Your lily-white sister should be just the one."

I couldn't hear Father's reply, but Claudine came back with, "Yes, such an example. Let us not forget . . ."

They both must have been at the other end of the verandah because I couldn't make out any words after that. Soon their conversation turned into a shouting match; that much I could tell. There might even have been a slap . . . it sounded like it. I do know that Father slept on the living room sofa that night.

Neither of them ever mentioned the quarrel to me. In the days that followed everything seemed more or less normal, though subdued. I'd tucked the incident 'way in the back of my mind and hadn't let myself think of it again until now.

Sighing, I tossed the book aside. I got out a sheet of scented stationery Claudine had given me before I left.

Dear, darling Rajee,

I began.

I do miss you so dreadfully.

What next?

Here alone, in my sad little room

What?

I am thinking of the day

What day?

we strolled through the gardens and . . .

Oh, really. A letter to one's beloved shouldn't be such an awful strain to write. I'd put it off. Perhaps tomorrow his first letter would arrive and that would serve as inspiration.

Right now I'd take a warm bath and relax, so I'd be better able to absorb that blasted reading assignment.

The Scarlet Letter. The lily-white aunt. What a strange combination to be in my mind all at once. I could do well without either of them.

Chapter Eight

There was no letter from Rajee the next day nor the next. Then, when I'd grown truly hopeless, there it was in the mailbox, a thin airmail envelope with his strange but beautiful handwriting on it.

Aunt Meg wasn't home yet, but I raced to my room and closed the door anyway. I slammed down my books, lit a joss stick and sat cross-legged on the floor in front of the curling smoke.

I inhaled and exhaled several times, intoning my mantra and holding the precious envelope against my chest. I was too excited, though, for the sense of peace and tranquility to come through so I gave up and ripped open the envelope.

My dear, my precious dove,

he began. My heart began fluttering like wings.

Since you have flown into the blue heavens all joy and delight have departed from this life.

This wasn't going to be a poem, then, but the straight stuff.

I grow listless with longing for your fair face. Even my friends notice and say, "Poor Rajee, he will die of love."

I knew this was most likely not the case, but it was sweet of Rajee to pretend.

> *And Lindsay? She does not write. She has no mercy for this heartsick guy.*

"Guy" was a word Rajee had picked up from an old James Cagney movie. He used it a lot.

> *And so what must I think? Has she forgotten her Rajee so soon? This Lindsay who not so long ago declared her undying love?*

Had I declared that? I guess I had. We'd both said a lot during the pain of parting.

> *So if you receive this poor letter, take pity on one who loves you so dearly. Write and say you too tremble with longing and such sadness as I have. But if already you have forgotten me and now love some American guy do not say so in a letter or I shall surely kill myself.*
> *I will leave with these tender emotions.*
>
> > *Love always,*
> > *your Rajee*

Ohhhhh . . . poor Rajee. The poor darling. He thought I'd forgotten. But perhaps at this very moment my first letter was in his hands.

Considering the differences in time, though . . . well, he might be sleeping with my letter next to his cheek.

I jumped at the sound of the garage door closing. Feeling foolishly guilty I leaned forward and thrust the letter under the bedspread, then returned to the yoga position.

I sensed, rather than heard, Aunt Meg coming down the carpeted hall. I knew she'd paused outside my door and I waited for her tenative rap.

"Yes?" I answered when it sounded. "Come in."

She opened the door a crack. "Oh, I'm sorry," she said. The fumes . . . Jasmine-scented this time . . . must have hit her full blast. "It can wait."

"No, no." I scrambled to my feet. "I was through anyway. What's up?" (Kids here were always saying that.)

"Lindsay, I'm really sorry to make this so late, but I thought . . . Eliot thought we might go out to dinner together. He's at a meeting with a client near here."

"Oh." The last thing I wanted to do was go out this evening when I was in so blissful a mood. "I wish I could, Aunt Meg, but during study hall I couldn't . . . I mean, I have this test coming up. . . ."

"Oh, I know it's unexpected. At least, though, you'll get to meet Eliot."

"I'd love that." Now that I had a letter from Rajee I could love anything. "Don't worry about dinner for me. I'm not hungry. I'll find something later."

When she went off to her room it occurred to me what I'd do this evening. I'd call. What a splendid idea! It was my phone. My money.

How much did I have, though?

I got out the red zippered case and counted the dollars. One hundred and twenty-one. There was also roughly thirty dollars in rupee notes I'd forgotten to change. A nice stack of money it was.

Father had told me to buy anything I needed instantly with the cash and then to charge other things and send him the bills. Aunt Meg had insisted on paying, though. Well, let the two of them sort it out. I didn't care. In the meantime, I had quite enough money for one little call to India.

It seemed as though Aunt Meg would never get ready,

and when she finally did . . . looking quite chic in a silk dress and pearls (real onces, I could tell) . . . Eliot kept her waiting. He called twice, though, and finally arrived.

I don't know what I expected . . . a proper business type with perhaps a mustache, I suppose. Eliot was anything but that. For starters, he swooped me up in what is called a bear hug, called me *sweetie*, and asked if I was, by any chance, a hockey fan.

"What sort of fan is that?" I asked, truly confused.

"Oh, Eliot." Aunt Meg wriggled back into the pumps she'd kicked off earlier. "The universe isn't full of sports nuts like you."

"Like me?" Eliot put a hand on his chest in mock surprise. "Madam, let me point out . . ."

"Later. Lindsay, hon, I won't be out late. But if you mind being alone, I'll bet Ruthanne . . ."

"No, no, I'll be fine," I said, still smiling at Eliot. He was a teddy bear sort of guy, with dark, rumply hair and hazel eyes.

"Hey, it's great meeting you at last," he said, an arm casually draped over my shoulder as I walked them to the door, "Pay no attention to the bad press. I'm really a very normal, congenial fellow."

"I can tell that," I said.

"See?" he said over my head to Meg. And just before they left, "We'll all have to get together soon. Okay?"

"Great!" I said, in the same American manner. "Bye."

I wandered about restlessly for a while . . . turned the TV on and off . . . looked in the refrigerator. What time was it now? A bit past eight. I'd wait until about nine to call.

68

But as time dragged on I began to lose my courage. What if I called and *she* answered . . . Rajee's mother? Or one of his possessive sisters? They despised me, and for no good reason except that their one and only brother so obviously adored me.

Well, perhaps *obviously* wasn't quite the word. I sat on the sofa, swirling the ice around in my Pepsi. Rajee's behavior toward me was proper if not downright stand-offish around his family. In fact, the only time he'd turned white-lipped in anger toward me was after I'd impulsively leaned over and kissed his cheek, in front of his sisters.

"You must never kiss me . . . touch me . . . in public again," he said later in a most chilly manner.

"Public! Surely your sisters . . ."

"Never!"

I tilted the glass for the last ice cube, which I crunched. Now that I thought about it, Rajee wasn't that affectionate even when we were alone. Maybe he thought all of India was bugged, like in spy movies. His poems were so full of passion, though. There are probably, I thought, things about even a loved one that a person doesn't quite understand.

But getting back to the phone call — What did I want? To hear Rajee's voice? To let him know I was thinking of him, just in case my letters to him had gone astray either by chance or design. If I called his home, though, and someone else answered, Rajee might never know that I phoned.

I got hungry. I went out and made a peanut butter and jelly sandwich and poured a huge glass of milk. Halfway through this banquet the idea came of what I should do. I'd call my father's bungalow.

If Claudine were back and answered I'd ask her to get the message to Rajee. She'd do it, of course, being the true romantic.

If my father answered I'd work on the guilt angle. Surely he was feeling pangs by now, sending his only child off across the seas? I'd cry a bit and say, "Father, Rajee and I are so far apart (thanks to you). At least you can tell him I'm thinking of him and have written. Is that so much to ask?"

While I had Father on the line I could also ask if he and Claudine were still separated. If such were the case, I could come home to keep him company. If Claudine's influence was thought to be detrimental . . . well, she was no longer around to corrupt the innocent. I missed Claudine, but I also missed Father most dreadfully at times. He seemed stern on the surface, but he had a gentle heart. I knew I mustn't dwell on all that, though; the thing to do was place the call.

It took a bit of doing, but eventually I heard the telephone ringing. How extraordinary! I was hearing sounds from the bungalow back home! Finally I heard a voice.

"Hello, who is this?" I shouted.

"Who this is?" Silence. "Who this is calling?"

"Sudha?" It could be her, the maid.

"Sudha no is here. Sudha sister, she get marry, she no here today, thank you good-bye."

"No, wait! Who is this?" I was sweating. And seeing money roll down the drain. "This is Lindsay. Who is speaking?"

"Lindsay! Oh, it not possible! *Baba* Lindsay, you come back to old *ayah*?"

"Is this Hamida? Hamida, is my father there?"

"*Baba* Lindsay, where you are? Come let *ayah* see you again, she most unhappy you go away so long time!"

Things were clearly getting out of control. Speaking slowly and distinctly, I said, "*Ayah* Hamida, I am far away. I am . . ." What? How to explain? "Sweet *ayah*, I want to speak to my father."

"My father?"

"Sahib Collins. Get Sahib for me. To talk on phone."

"Oh, *Baba*, no talk. Sahib not here."

"Well, then. Get Memsahib. Tell her Lindsay wants to talk to her."

"Memsahib?"

"Yes. Please."

"She no here too. Memsahib away. She go and leave wicked Sudha here to make so sad your *ayah*. Oh, that wicked Sudha, she tell boy this morning, 'You cheat. You no bring good vegetable, you no bring the thing I most certainly ask, and the boy, he said to wicked Sudha . . .'"

"Hamida . . . when will my father . . . when will Sahib Collins be back?"

"Sahib? He no here."

I wanted to scream. "Tell him I called. Tell him. Say 'Lindsay called.' You understand?"

"You come back? You leave most desolate your faithful . . ."

"I'll be back. I have to hang up now, Hamida. Tell my father. Please. Good-bye."

And I hung up, severing the connection as well as severing myself from untold dollars. What a waste the call had been. Well, not a total waste. I'd learned one thing at least. Claudine was indeed gone. But was she *gone*? Or just out for the evening? No, morning. What had I said? What exactly had Hamida said? I couldn't remember!

I got another Pepsi, held it against my warm forehead for a moment, then gulped straight from the can. Walking back to the living room I tried to make some sense of the conversation. Claudine had left Sudha in charge. But for how long? Even an hour was too long as far as Hamida was concerned. And I wasn't around to hear her complaints.

Poor *ayah*. She must miss me a lot even though I wasn't exactly a rose in her garden of life.

She'd come faithfully to my door each morning when there was school, bringing me wake-up tea and braving the verbal abuse I invariably flung at her.

"Oh, *Baba* Lindsay," the old woman would sorrowfully exclaim, "such an angry way to greet your faithful Hamida."

If I was in a particularly vile mood I'd fling more than abuse, and she'd back toward the door, shaking her head and muttering in some dialect I couldn't understand. She never complained to Father, though. If I'd been exceedingly disagreeable I'd buy her a bangle next time I went to market. She had quite a string of them by the time I left.

Suddenly, sitting there, the tears started flowing. I was so alone! Father far away and Claudine who knew where? I wanted my *ayah* to take me into her arms and rock me back and forth and smooth my hair and tell me how good and sweet and totally marvelous I was. I wanted to be back in India. Home.

It would never be home here. Never. It was strange and unfriendly and cold, and the people nearest to me weren't near at all right now.

Even Jess, who had always been there to comfort and understand in other days was now somewhat indifferent. Aunt Meg, who at the moment would be better than no one at all, had gone out with that guy. Deserted me in my time of need. What did she care? She hadn't asked that I be dumped into her life, had she? Of course not. Why did she need me, an unknown niece? She had this super job that made her some kind of celebrity, she had her own house, her own friends. Her own . . . what? What was Eliot to her? Friend? Boyfriend? Lover? I frankly didn't care.

All I wanted was to go home. Home. But where in my life was home now?

Chapter Nine

Before coming here I hadn't really thought much about what it would be like. For one thing, I was used to moving about and for another, the pang of parting with Rajee was uppermost in my mind.

I'd simply assumed that I'd take up again with Jess, being his best friend and all, and that we'd share our memories of other places, other times.

Such turned out not to be the case. Jess was always busy it seemed, and seldom in the mood to dwell on old adventures. I felt quite cut off.

One day after school I saw him standing out by the curb, and stopping, asked, "What's up?"

"Just waiting for Hope." There was an awkward pause and then he said, "I heard about Claudine and your dad. How come you didn't mention it to me?"

"Because they're in India. And you don't want to hear anything about . . ."

"Hey, not so. Come on, Lindsay."

"Come on yourself. You know it's a fact."

"Look, Lindsay, I've got problems, but that doesn't mean . . ."

I could tell by the flush on his face that he was hurt and also embarrassed. "Well, sorry," I mumbled.

He cleared his throat. "What's with Rajee?"

"Oh, Rajee. Nothing. But then I'm not even sure he's getting my letters. You see, lately . . . oh, here's Hope."

Hope's Trans Am stopped in front of us. She leaned over, rolled down the window and said, "Hi, Lindsay. Hop in. Hi, Jess."

"I'd better just go . . ." I said.

"Nonsense. Jess, make her come with us."

"You heard them orders," Jess said in his sheriff voice from the old Westerns. "Move along now, little lady."

So I got in. We went to a drive-in, only inside, for Cokes and fries. For a while we talked about general things, school and all, and then Hope mentioned that her father might take flying lessons. "He wants my mom to take them, too, but I told him I wasn't ready to be an orphan."

"Flying's pretty safe," Jess said.

"That depends," I said. "Remember that time we flew to the game reserve, Jess?"

"Do I ever!"

He turned to Hope. "We flew there in some plane that looked stuck together with the Indian version of Crazy Glue. And we landed on grass. Grass!"

"Oh, and remember the terminal?" I said, delighted that Jess was acting like his old self. "Hope, it was a roof held up by bamboo poles, I'm not kidding, and just wooden benches."

"It was neat, though, the way the locals were ranged in a line, blowing on those flutes they play when charming snakes."

"I don't think they were the same," I said. This led into a discussion, until suddenly I noticed . . . and Jess did, too, that Hope was sitting there with a glazed look.

"Well, enough of all that," Jess said. "Hope, can our team really count on winning the . . .

And off they went on sports talk, little caring that now *I* was bored.

Jess must have felt a twinge of guilt, though. He called later that night, and for a change we had a good long chat. Now that we seemed on a friendly footing again I could even say that I liked Hope and wanted to be friends.

"No problem. She likes you. Really. Hold on a second, will you?" I heard him say something to Aunt Janice. "Hey, Lindsay, I have to run an errand. What was it about Rajee that you wanted to tell me?"

"Oh . . . nothing important. Just that we're out of touch."

"You ought to put Rajee on hold, anyway," he said, "and give the guys around here a break."

"I don't know what you mean."

"Sure you do. I've tried to fix you up a couple of times but you always . . ."

"That's a disgusting turn of phrase. *Fix you up*. I don't need fixing up, Jess."

"Okay. It's your funeral. I gotta go study now."

"Then go."

Jess would be sorry. Sorry when I went back to India and he'd lost forever the best friend he'd ever had.

On Sundays, after we'd had a leisurely brunch and lounged around reading the papers, Meg would take me any place I wanted to go. We went to museums and places of interest that even kids who lived right here hadn't seen.

It was nice of her, but sometimes I wished she'd just relax. It was as though she was trying to stack up points, like kids do with teachers sometimes . . . pretending great interest and all. But who was going to grade her in the course called Concern for Houseguests 101?

On this particular Sunday, I could sense Aunt Meg studying me as I frowned over an account of intrigue in one of our embassies. It disconcerted me when she did that. I mean, what was she trying to fathom, quietly watching me that way?

I faked a yawn and tossed the paper aside. "What's up for today?"

In a seemingly off-hand manner she said, "You know, there's an import shop that I check out every now and then. Want to run over? They might have a bedspread you'd like. Or something. They're always getting things from 'way off somewhere."

I didn't quite know what to say. I hoped I hadn't offended her by folding up the floral bedspread and stashing it in the closet. I did want some bright things . . . the room could certainly bear a bit of smartening up. But I didn't want her to pay for it. On the other hand, I wanted to have cash to cover that ill-fated phone call when the bill arrived. "It wouldn't hurt to look, I guess. If you're sure . . ."

"I'm sure." She flipped the paper aside and got up. "I'll just change out of this robe. It'll be fun . . . just you and me. I love going to that shop. It's so exotic."

"Shall I change?"

"Oh, no. Jeans are fine."

While she was off changing the front doorbell rang. It was Ruthanne and two of her friends.

"Oh, hi!" she said brightly. "What are you doing?"

"Getting ready to go out."

"Oh, good, glad we got here in time." She came in and the girls followed. "This is Tiffany and this is Gloria."

"Hi," I said. "I'm Lindsay."

"Is Aunt Meg around?" Ruthanne asked, with a strange look of pride. "Of the *Meg and Murray Show?*" The girls looked awed.

"She's changing. We're going out," I repeated.

"Oh. Oh! Here she is!" Ruthanne said as my aunt came out, still fastening her belt. "Hi, Aunt Meg!"

"Ruthanne . . ." She checked an earring. "How nice to see you."

"Aunt Meg, these are my friends. Tiffany and Gloria."

"Hello," she said, shaking their hands. "You're class-mates?"

"Yes, they are," Ruthanne said. "And also big fans of yours."

"Really. How nice." She raised an eyebrow in an amused way. "But surely you don't hear me. Aren't you in school?"

The girls giggled and hunched their shoulders. Finally the brunette one said, "I hear you when I'm home with asthma."

"Oh, dear. Sorry to hear that."

"And my mom listens to you all the time," the other said. "She couldn't believe it when I told her you lived here, and that Ruthanne knows you."

"Related," Ruthanne said.

I gave her a look that said, *you are not related.*

"They want your autograph," Ruthanne said.

"Oh, surely . . ."

"Please!" The brunette dug a piece of paper from her purse and at her friend's request, tore it in half. "I collect autographs," she said. "I got Johnny Cash's down at Nash-ville last year."

"I'm greatly flattered," Aunt Meg said. "Let's see now,

you're Gloria . . ." She pushed her hair behind her ear as she leaned over the hall table to scribble their names and hers. The girls didn't take their eyes off her.

I must confess that these girls, wimps though they were (Ruthanne included), made me see my aunt with different eyes. I suddenly realized that beyond this person who behaved so casually around the house lay a well-known public personality. Out in the world Aunt Meg was actually looked upon with awe.

"I certainly do thank you for dropping around," Aunt Meg said as she handed back the scraps of paper.

"It's okay," Gloria murmured.

"I guess we'd better get going," Ruthanne said. "Come on, guys. See you later, Aunt Meg." They left.

"You must get tired of that," I mumbled. "Signing your name."

"Oh, it doesn't happen often." Aunt Meg checked her purse for the keys and off we went.

The export store was really great. For one thing, instead of the mindless music they hit you with in grocery stores this one had African tribal chants going. And the place smelled of incense. Sandalwood. My favorite; incense of champions. I loaded up on a few more packs. Meg was really nice about just following me around while I handled brassware, sniffed at scented candles, and tried out various bamboo chairs.

"You really love that one, don't you?" she said as I kept going back to the chair with wide woven arms and a tremendous arching back. "Why don't we just get it?"

It cost $89.95. I had already bought a madras bedspread and the incense. "I'd better think about it," I said.

"But . . . if you like it so much?" She moistened her lips.

"Look, if it's the money . . . I'm getting it for you. Call it a settling-in gift. I'd like to. Really. And now's the time . . . it's on sale."

"But what would you do with it when . . ." Something made me stop. *When I go back home* was what I'd been about to say. "When . . . my things arrive?" And then, since I really did want it so much, "Of course, I don't have a chair like this."

"Then it's settled." She walked over to a sales clerk.

Okay. I'd let her buy it. She'd be hurt if I didn't. And I had to keep my money for that blasted phone bill. I just hoped it would come separately from hers. I was feeling closer to Aunt Meg but not *that* close. If she found out now about the call it would be rather awkward to explain why I hadn't mentioned it before.

When we got back to the house there was a red car sitting in our driveway.

"Hey, that's Eliot's Chevy," Aunt Meg said. "What gives?"

He wasn't in it, and obviously wasn't in the house, since Aunt Meg said herself that he didn't have a key.

"Maybe he's down at Uncle Robert's," I said. I knew Eliot knew them because Ruthanne frequently raved about what a "super guy" he was and even Jess, when I quizzed him privately, admitted that Eliot was good-natured as well as being bright.

We strolled down to the McIntyres' house. Even before we saw the driveway beyond the trees we heard the thump of the basketball and a voice, not Jess's, yelling, "Lucky shot . . . dumb luck!" followed by laughter.

"Hey, you sports!" Aunt Meg called when they got into

view. Eliot turned, yelled, "Hey yourself!" and arched the ball to Aunt Meg, who caught it against her middle with an *oomph.*

"Come on, Aunt Meg, long shot!" Jess yelled. "Show the champ how it's done!"

She tried, but the ball fell short of the net. Eliot caught it on the bounce and jogged over to us. "Hi, sweetie," he said, giving Meg a kiss. "And Lindy-Lou . . ." He kissed me on both cheeks in the continental manner because for whatever reason he always pretended I was French.

"How long have you been here?" Meg asked. "If we'd known . . ."

"We wouldn't have come back so soon," I said, grinning. He was the first adult I'd ever met who seemed to thrive on insults. Still, I didn't know him all that well yet.

He patted the top of my head. "I had to run some papers out to a client in Northlake so I thought I'd swing by here and check out the action."

"A client?" Meg looked at his gray sweat outfit and running shoes. "And what is his line of business . . . manager of Sports World?"

"You're close. Don't you remember my mentioning Jensen, that old army buddy of mine?"

"Vaguely."

"Sure you do. He's the one who helped me run that lottery I was telling you about. Great business head. Anyway, he's rolling in it now and insists I handle all his investments. Which I graciously do, his being a buddy and all."

"Aha. The spoils of war." Aunt Meg jangled her car keys. "Are you tied up for the rest of the afternoon here or do you want to come over to the house?"

"You'd better knock it off," Jess said to Eliot. "At your age . . ."

Eliot turned and pitched the ball at Jess. "Young savage! Wait 'til I get you in a handball court. I'll show you *old!*"

Jess laughed and went back to tossing at the net. I was wondering if I should stay or what, but Eliot put an arm around Meg's shoulder and the other around mine and we strolled back down the street. "Where've you gals been?"

We told him. He whistled when he saw the chair in the rear of the car. "Lucky you have a hatch-back. And lucky you found a strapping lad to haul it in for you."

Although I'd talked to Eliot on the phone only a few times and seen him on only two or maybe three occasions, I was already used to his way of kidding around about most things. It was hard for me to believe he was an investment broker, but Aunt Meg said he was good at it. Maybe he jollied his clients around and got them so relaxed they lost sight of the hard business facts.

"So, ladies," he said after he'd placed the chair in my room, "what is your pleasure? Would you allow me to take you to some nifty joint for dinner?"

Aunt Meg eyed his outfit. "Even Taco Bell is out. Come on, let's check the freezer. I know we have steaks."

"I could make brownies," I said. "Remember, we bought that kind where you just add water and eggs?"

"Homemade pastries!" Eliot rolled his eyes. "This child is a regular Julia Child. What next, I wonder?"

"For starters," Meg said, "while Lin makes the brownies, you, Eliot, can make a set of margaritas. I'm going in to change. I feel shockingly overdressed next to you two."

*

We ate in the dining room. Candlelight, wine, the works. I even drank a bit of wine without getting the least bit tiddly.

If I'd known in advance that the three of us would be spending these hours together I might have been a bit tense, or even scooted over to Jess's. But it had all happened naturally. It was a first for me, being around adults who were easy, relaxed, and accepting. With Father and Claudine there was always a bit of a strain, as though Father was watching to see which of us would erupt into a bit of childish behavior that would annoy and embarrass him in front of the servants.

Here, now, I didn't doubt that if I did something totally out of line, Aunt Meg's and even Eliot's attitude would change. But I had no desire to do anything of the sort. I was content. And happy. I couldn't remember ever having been happy in this way before — not with grownups.

Chapter Ten

"But this is odd," Aunt Meg said, going through her mail at the kitchen table after dinner one evening. "We've been billed for a call to India earlier this month and I didn't . . .

"Oh," I said with a lightness I didn't feel, "that must be the call *I* made. I'll pay for it, of course."

"*You* made?" Meg's eyes were fixed on me.

"Yes, it was one evening you were out. I got lonesome for my father, so I just called. As you know, he seldom writes."

"Lindsay," she said, her eyes never straying, "You know you're free to call if you need to or want to. But I wonder why you didn't mention it."

To keep from seeing her hurt, questioning look I got up and started clearing the table. "It turned into a real bummer," I said, employing a handy new bit of slang. "No one was home but Hamida . . . my old *ayah* . . . and she was so shook up I didn't find out a thing."

"What was it you were trying to find out, Lindsay?"

What a slip. From lonesome to inquisitive. "I was just . . . uh . . . wondering if Father and Claudine were still separated. Do you happen to know?" Why hadn't I simply asked Meg, then? This wasn't going well at all.

Aunt Meg poured herself some coffee. "I haven't heard

either. If you're so concerned I suggest you write to your father and ask, very specifically."

"All right, I will. But don't worry. I'll *pay* for that call!" I really hadn't meant for that little sarcastic edge, so much like Claudine's, to creep into my voice.

For a moment Aunt Meg just looked at me. Then she got up. The cup and saucer rattled slightly as she walked toward the door.

"I'm . . . sorry," I said. "I really didn't mean . . ."

"It's all right." But she kept going, and didn't come back.

Oh, now you've done it, I said to myself as I cleared up the dishes. Gone and hurt her feelings when she'd done nothing to deserve it. But what about *my* feelings? Did anyone ever ask if I was hurting from loneliness and abandonment? Never.

And Rajee. Whatever was going on with him? How was I supposed to feel when my true love writes one letter full of desire and passion. I reply in kind . . . several times . . . and what do I receive in return? A letter so impersonal it could have been written by a pen pal.

Although I could recite it from memory, I took out the letter once again when I got back to my room. It read just the same:

Dear Friend:

What had happened to his little dove, then? Flown away?

It has been some time now since you have left.

Yes, I do know that.

Life is most quiet and dull.

Good!

I am playing still quite a lot of soccer and tennis. But mostly I prepare for the examinations, so there is little to say. My sisters send their greetings,

Oh, sure!

as does my mother.

Rajee, you know that is an out-and-out-lie.

So until next time I will say adieu and hope to hear from you soon.
                                    Lovingly, your Rajee

Lovingly, your Rajee. The only part of the letter worth the postage.

It didn't make sense. How could he have grown so cold so quickly? What had happened to change his mood?

Could someone . . . his monstrous mother, for instance . . . have got hold of my letters to him? If so, why didn't he write and warn me to tone them down a bit?

A sudden thought struck. What if Rajee had gone on to assume Aunt Meg censored my mail? Of course! That was it!

Aunt Meg appeared in the hall, dressed for bed. Impulsively, I went out and hugged her. "I'm sorry. Truly."

She kissed the top of my head and leaned her chin on me for a moment. "Look, I had a bad day. That's mainly it."

I pulled away. "I should have told you, though. About the call."

"Lindsay, it's all right. You needn't get permission for these things, you know. I'm not your . . . your jailer."

She was so nice, and so understanding. I was tempted to tell her about all the things that were troubling me. But I still didn't know, really, why I'd been sent here. And I didn't know, if it came to a showdown, whose side Meg would be on.

The next Saturday I got Jess to drive me to the bank. On the way I told him about Rajee's sudden reversal of attitudes and my suspicions. "In short," I said, "I believe my letters are being intercepted. And Rajee, not believing that *land of the free business* suspects the same is going on here. So Jess, it might be well if *you* wrote to Rajee."

"Me?" He shot me a quick look. "What for?"

"They wouldn't suspect anything from you. His family, I mean. And anyway, you could word the letter in such a casual way, you know, that he might write back and give you the scoop." I was pleased at how I'd worked *scoop* into ordinary talk.

"I don't know. I'd have to think about it. What bank did you say?"

"It doesn't matter. Some big one, I expect."

"I thought you and Hope were going shopping today."

"We are. That's why I need the money."

Jess stopped for a light. "What did you think of the guy I introduced you to?"

"Which one was that?" I yawned.

"Which one? Cary. Remember? Yesterday."

"Oh, yes. A bit on the conceited side, I thought."

"You thought. Did it ever occur to you, Lindsay, that maybe you aren't perfect, yourself?"

"I've never thought I was, Jess. At least not in every way."

"You . . ." He stopped, shook his head and laughed. "You're impossible!"

"Now, Jess, you know that I'm not impossible. And if I am, it's surely the way I was brought up, and not my fault at all."

"Lindsay, I'm just telling you that you should be more open, make friends. Now, I know you're not a snob . . ."

"Thanks so much."

". . . but other people don't know you as I do. You don't give them a chance."

I was thinking that I'd never needed to make friends before. I always had Jess. "You may find this hard to believe, Jess," I said, "But I'm a bit frightened of meeting new people."

"I believe it. I am too. But it gets easier the more you try. Now, Cary, for instance. He'd like to take you out, but you've got to . . ."

"I'm not much interested in going out. Unless it would be on a strictly friendship basis."

"Cary's not looking to get engaged, Lindsay. He just thinks you'd be fun to go out with. Gee!"

"Do you ever think of getting married, Jess? I mean, seriously?"

"No. I've got too many years ahead of me at college. I'm getting really interested in biology . . . plant management. Did I tell you?"

"I don't think so. The light's changing."

"I see it. I guess living overseas and realizing what just one crop failure can do to a country . . ."

"Your dad was talking about that too."

"Yeh, it's a serious world problem. He's getting into the farm implement trade and crop experiments. . . ."

"That bank looks okay. That one ahead."

"All right." He hesitated at the entrance. "Can this be handled at the drive-in window?"

"I don't know."

He looked a bit annoyed. "Well, what is it you have to do? Cash a check, open a savings account or what?"

"I want to convert my rupees into dollars."

"Your *what?*"

"Rupees, rupees, Jess. What's the matter?"

"Dummy, you can't do that at just any bank. In fact, I doubt you can do it at any. Is that what we drove over here for?"

I could feel tears about to start. Jess had never called me *dummy* before. "What's wrong with changing money? We did it everywhere in India! Why can't I . . . ?"

"Banks here aren't equipped to convert money from just any place into dollars."

"India isn't *just anyplace!*"

"You know yourself that American dollars are good in lots of countries and easy to change. But here it doesn't work . . ."

"Well, I think that's beastly. Just another example of American arrogance." I began to cry out of frustration.

Jess's voice softened. "Linny, I'm sorry. I'll get Dad to change the bills for you. And in the meantime, if you want to borrow . . . Come on, don't cry. It's only money."

I wiped away the tears. "It's not just the money, Jess, it's my whole life. I'm not sure of anything anymore. Did you know that Father and Claudine are getting a divorce?"

Jess went through the bank exit and started back home. "No, I didn't know that. Are you sure?"

"It looks like it. Of course, no one tells *me* anything. I'm like a step-child, sent away because I muddle things up."

"Where did you get that?"

I ignored his question and plunged on. "And now, the only person I truly love, to whom I plighted my troth, is probably afraid to write!"

"If you think it will help, I'll drop Rajee a note."

"I'm thinking I'll just go back and sneak into the country and meet him and elope."

"That's what you're thinking, huh?"

"Rajee and I could go to Srinagar in the Vale of Kashmir. Rent one of those splendid houseboats for our honeymoon." I took out mirror and comb. "Remember when we were there that time?"

"Yeh." He headed for home. "Anywhere else you want to go?"

"Agra. Rajee and I could go to Agra. Get married at the Taj Mahal."

"I meant *now*. Anyway, the Taj Mahal, as you well know, is a mausoleum. Not a wedding chapel."

We had reached our driveway. "Jess, do you think that we'll ever see the Taj Mahal by moonlight? You know they say . . ."

"I know. But I can't see it happening. Not for me . . . not very soon." He leaned over and kissed my cheek in a brotherly way.

"Jess, do you know, you're the only person in all the world to whom I can say about the Taj . . . *remember when?* No one else will ever know exactly what it was like."

Jess rested his hands on the wheel. "There'll be other places and times, Lindsay. With other people."

"I seriously doubt that. Jess, what are you looking at?"

His gaze was riveted on the rearview mirror. "Hope's there, behind us. I wonder how long . . ."

"Okay, I'll hurry." I reached for the door handle. "Thanks for taking me to the bank, even though . . ." but Jess was out and walking back toward Hope's car. I don't know what he said in the moment or two before I got in but it must have been all right because Hope was saying, "I understand. See you later."

I didn't see any great need to review what Jess and I had said or explain what might have looked like a tender scene. All I did was tell Hope about the rupee notes, making rather a joke of it. Off we went to the shopping mall.

Hope was patience itself as she took me from one teen shop to another in search of summer clothes. I saw quite a few things that I really liked but still I pretended that they weren't quite the thing.

"If you'd tell me what you have in mind . . ." Hope held out a peach-colored embroidered top. "Don't you like this? I think it's darling."

Actually, it would have looked better on her than me. My complexion called for cooler shades. "I should have told you before," I said. "Right now I'm short of money so I thought I'd just look around for ideas. Then I'll write to my father to see if he'll cough up the cash."

"I wish I could do that with my dad," Hope said. "Only I can't."

"You can't?" (I still said *cahn't*) "Didn't your father buy you the car?"

"Yes, but he's lowering the boom. Says I have to get a

job this summer and start spending my own money on clothes."

A job? I hadn't thought of that. "What sort of job would you get?"

"I don't have much choice. Jobs are scarce. Most college kids spent last Christmas vacation lining up jobs for this summer. But my father knows someone in, would you believe, a Chinese restaurant? So that's what I'll be doing. Slinging chop suey."

"You're making me hungry. Shall we break for lunch?"

Hope looked at the heavy digital watch on her wrist. It was a man's watch but it looked good on her. "It's already two-thirty. Okay if we just hit McDonald's?"

"Sure." It was great, actually, since I was going to insist on paying. I still had enough money for the common decencies.

Just as we were going toward the counter a hand touched my arm, and a voice said, "I can't believe it!"

I whirled. For a moment I just stared at the girl, and then . . . "Krissy!"

"Lindsay! I thought it was you. Hey, how's it goin'?"

"Great. Krissy, I just can't believe it!"

She looked away and called to a group of kids, "Hold it for a minute, you guys!" And then, "So how do you like it here?"

"Fine. Oh, Krissy, this is Hope Chang, a friend of mine." And I explained to Hope how Krissy and I had met on the plane.

"You know, Bones and I were just talking about you the other day. The way you put on the sari? That was a riot."

"Uh. Did you make up with your boyfriend?"

"Jimmy? No. I'm going out with Michael now. Tell me, how's that cute boyfriend of yours? The one in the snapshot?

"Rajee's fine. Misses me."

"Uh, no. I meant the other one . . . that you said was already over here? The cute one that you knew so well and all?"

"Oh, that one." I wanted to fade away into the crowds. I didn't dare look at Hope. "He's . . . fine, I guess. Well, it's certainly great seeing you. . . . Tell Bones I said hello."

"Sure." Krissy gave me a sort of puzzled look and started away. "See you around!"

It was lucky I was ahead of Hope as we moved in the line toward the counter because I could feel my face flaming. Twice in one day. It was incredible. What could I possibly say . . . now?

We ordered, and I almost dropped the money in my hurry to pay. Hope made a token objection but allowed it. As we ate, she made only necessary comments as I prattled on and on, mindlessly, about the trip coming over and the way the kids had lived it up on the plane.

I really just wanted to run and hide as I had done as a child when things went wrong. But I knew that unless I said something now I'd lose Hope as a friend, and perhaps Jess as well.

Working the straw back and forth in the ice chips, I finally said, "I know what you're thinking, Hope, but it isn't so."

She raised her eyebrows slightly but didn't answer.

"I never told Krissy that Jess was my boyfriend. I don't think of him that way at all. I never have."

She made a little sound.

"He was just the only one I could talk to at times. Still the only one. My father hasn't written or called, even though I left a message."

"You haven't heard from him at all?"

"No. He's all right. Uncle Robert said the other day, 'Oh, Lindsay, your father asked about you and said to tell you *hello*.' Isn't that splendid? Nice that he remembered."

"He's probably upset. Are he and what's-her-name still separated?"

"Claudine. Yes, I expect so. Still, without me around for them to argue about, who knows?" I shrugged. "No one tells me anything."

"Maybe Rajee could get the scoop for you. Did you ever think of that?"

"Oh, Rajee. There's another strange one. He's written twice. Just twice in all this time. While I must have sent a dozen. . . ."

"I don't get it," Hope said, frowning. "What's going on over there, anyway?"

"That's what I'd like to know. Jess said he'd try to find out. . . . That's what we were talking about in the car. But I truly think I'll have to run over there myself."

"You do? But where would you get the money? It's got to cost a mint . . . to India!"

"I'll manage. There's money in a savings account, if I can get my hands on it. Or it may be possible to charge the air fare with one of those plastic cards." I sighed deeply. "I've got to do something. I keep hearing voices chanting, *Lindsay, Lindsay, fly away home*."

Hope looked at me and shook her head. "You are one far-out number."

"No, actually, I'm quite normal. It's just that everyone seems to be going about with some sort of secret." I hadn't really thought that until I said it. But it was true. Father wasn't communicating. Rajee had turned strange and distant. Even Aunt Meg sometimes looked at me as though I were someone else . . . and seemed to be listening to something beyond what I was saying.

"It really *is* true," I said, starting to gather up the debris. "There seems to be some mysterious force at work in my life."

Hope gave the table a last little swipe with her napkin and followed me to the trash bin.

I shoved the stuff through the swinging lid. It swung back, flipping sticky ice chips all over the floor.

"Look! See what I mean?" I said. "Every*one* and every*thing*. What do we do?"

"Let the help handle it."

I followed Hope out. "I wish I had help for my other problems."

"You have, Lindsay. Time. Time heals all wounds. And wounds all heels, or so they say."

"Oh, Hope." She was kidding of course, but she might be right about the *time* thing. In time I should surely know the answers to my many perplexing problems. But I'd never been good about waiting.

Chapter Eleven

Summer was here, school was out, and I didn't know what to do with myself.

Oh, true, my social life, if you want to call it that, had picked up. I finally took Jess's advice and went out on dates, mostly doubles, to prove that I wasn't harboring some great, unrequitted passion for *him* — Jess. There was one chap, Jerry Winslowe, who wasn't too bad, but the one I hung out with most — and he was one of my own choosing — was Turk Trimball, a weird number in everyone else's eyes. I liked Turk for the very reason that he wasn't particularly popular with most of the crowd. In fact, *Turk* was a nickname, derivative of *Turkey,* which had been put upon him and which he minded not one whit.

"I know they call me Turk," he said to me one time, "as a way of putting me down. Fortunately, my ego structure is such that incidental and varied slurs only activate my interest in studying the motivations and machinations of the animal we call 'man.'"

"I quite agree," I said, not bothering in my mind to pare down what he'd said to basic English. Instead of his talk being irritating to me, as it was to some of the others, I found it peculiarly restful. I seldom truly listened. It was like turning a radio down at night so that the sounds are more like murmurs, but there to fill the void.

Another thing I liked about Turk was that he wasn't a gossip. (Of course, there weren't that many people who'd listen to him anyway.) If I felt like airing grievances, he listened. If I felt nostalgic about some time or place from my past, he took it seriously. There was no need to try to be witty and clever around Turk.

"What terminal are we headed for?" I asked Jess the next day as we drove to the airport to pick up his father.

"International, just up ahead. Dad's probably waiting out front. He'd already cleared customs when he called."

"I see him! Here, I'll divert that cab so you can swing over to the curb." I made a wild face at the driver and sure enough he paused long enough for Jess to pull in front of him. "There's Uncle Robert!"

Jess got out, shook hands with his father, and got the luggage into the trunk. I had finally learned not to call it the *boot*. I jumped out too. "Hi, there, Uncle!" We kissed and he insisted I sit in the front with them.

"So how was the trip?" Jess asked, cutting sharply into the traffic.

"Fine." Watch out for that limousine!"

"Dad . . ."

"All right, all right. How's your mother? Ruthanne?"

"Mom's fine. Ruthanne has a daytime job, baby-sitting."

"That's good. And Meg?"

"She's okay," I told him. "She and Murray have some new account to advertise, a dog food, and she's been busy meeting with the customers. I mean, the clients, not the dogs. Did you get to Bombay this trip?"

"Uh huh. Just a couple of days, though. How are you getting along with Eliot? Seen much of him?"

"Quite a bit. He's been busy too."

"Eliot's deceptive. He seems such an easygoing fellow. You'd think he didn't take anything seriously."

Why all this chitchat about Eliot? I wondered. If it was meant to distract me, it wouldn't work. "Did you see my father? And Claudine?"

"Yes, I did, as a matter of fact. Your father said to tell you he misses you a lot and wonders if you've turned into the sweet All-American Girl."

"Not bloody likely. Is Claudine back with him, then?"

"Yes, it seems they had a trial separation but now they're having . . ."

"A second honeymoon, I expect. With me not about." I don't know why the news hurt me; it just did.

Uncle Robert's reply was a mild, "They seem to be getting along well. Oh, and they sent gifts. They're in my bag."

"Did you see my old *ayah*?"

"Hamida? Did I ever. She was ranting and raving about her *baba*, how she misses you and so on. But she's fine."

"I must write to her." I gave a little sniff. "I wish I could have gone with you. I'm so homesick."

"You are? After so short a time?"

"Two months or more."

"Oh, honey, when you get to my age you'll find two months is like two breaths." His arm tightened about my shoulder. "But I know for kids it's different." He paused while Jess maneuvered into a turn-off lane. "So I'll tell you what was going to be a surprise . . . so you can look forward to it. Your father's planning on coming over next month."

"He is?" I looked at Uncle Robert. "For sure?"

"In this business you never know for sure. But Daniel says he wants to check out the corn situation with me."

"Corn?"

"The high-yield crop methods. If we could set up some of those procedures in underdeveloped countries . . ."

Jess slowed and flung coins into the toll bin. "I'd like to see how that's done, too, Dad. It's a field I might decide to study in college."

"No reason why you couldn't check it out, Jess. We'll be going downstate when the crop's ready. You're not tied into any job, are you?"

"Just the car wash. Three afternoons and weekends. The pay's lousy. Hope makes more money in tips in just one night."

"All right. We'll see. I'd like you to see some real farm country anyway."

Jess and Uncle Robert went on, then, talking about crops and farm implements and other subjects of not the slightest interest to me.

What I really wanted to know was *How did it feel back in India?* But Uncle Robert was one of those people who didn't react much to surroundings, just to the business at hand. And, of course, there was no use even asking about Rajee. Even if Uncle Robert knew anything . . . which I doubted . . . he wouldn't tell.

When they dropped me off I did ask, "Uncle Robert, do you happen to know why my father never returned a call I tried to make to him?"

For a moment Jess's dad seemed to have been caught off-guard. Then like the true diplomat he said, "That's something you'd better ask him when he gets here."

"I suppose so. Bye." I went into the house feeling even

more alone than usual. Everyone had someone they could talk to, who would give them answers. But no one told me anything.

One night Aunt Meg and I were sitting out on the verandah. She said here most people would say *screened-in porch* but she liked the nostalgic sound of *verandah* better. She was sitting in a white wicker chair next to a table, with her coffee and tape recorder. I was stretched out on the white wicker sofa with its plump floral cushions.

"Is this disturbing you?" she asked, clicking the off button. "I could go somewhere else."

"Oh, no. I was just thinking." I put my book on the woven mat floor. "Was it really like that in the old days?"

"What old days?" She clamped a pencil between her teeth and flipped to another page of her report.

"I was reading this book, *Dandelion Wine*, and it sounds like such a happy, peaceful kind of life."

"That was before my time, but yes, I do think it must have been like that. Especially in the Midwest. Ray Bradbury really gets the mood of it, doesn't he?"

"You've read it?"

"Oh, sure. A long time ago. I reread parts of it every now and then. You know one of the stories I really like? And think about every once in a while?"

"Which one?" I hoisted myself up a little.

"The one where the kids visit the old lady and she tries to tell them about what she was like as a young girl. . . ."

"And they won't believe she was ever young! I just read that one!"

"I find it so true, even of someone my age. I mean, I'll get to know some older person fairly well and no matter how hard I try, I can't picture him or her as ever being any way but the way they are now." She laughed. "Funny, huh?"

"Yes, it is." I sat up and folded one leg under me. "I can't picture my father, for instance, as a little kid who got dirty and was bratty sometimes."

"I don't know about dirty and bratty, but I can guarantee Daniel was a kid, like everyone else."

"Did you know my mother when she was little? My real mother?"

"Uh . . . no. I met Katherine in college. When she was going out with my brother. Daniel."

"What was she like, then?"

"Ummmm, pretty in a quiet sort of way. She planned to be a teacher, but then she married Daniel and they went overseas shortly after."

"Couldn't she have taught over there, in the American School?"

"Well . . . she had you to raise."

"I was born here, though. I'm an American citizen."

"Yes. They took you with them."

"Did you like her? Be honest now."

"Of course I liked her. Otherwise . . . Lindsay, did you ever ask your father these things?"

"I used to try. He'd just get sad or angry, though, so I stopped. There was something else he wouldn't talk about either."

"Oh? What?"

"Well, maybe I shouldn't mention it, but still, I've been ever so curious. I heard him talking to Claudine a long time ago. I can barely remember it, except for just one thing. It was about you."

"Me? Like what?" Something about her smile didn't look quite real.

"Just tell me it's none of my business if you like."

"Lindsay, come on now. What did he say?" She pushed back her hair. "Something really awful? Let's hear."

"Not awful. Sad, really. He said something about your tragic love affair."

"Oh, really. And what was it he said about it?"

"Well, that's it, you see. I don't remember. Or maybe I never heard. But I've been dying to know about it ever since. Not all the time, but now and then."

"I was very young. In college. And very much in love. With your Uncle Robert's brother, as a matter of fact."

"No kidding. What happened?"

"He died." She picked up the report again, flipped through the pages, and frowned, but I had the feeling she wasn't reading. I also had the feeling that this was the end of the conversation.

I picked up the paperback and turned pages, but I wasn't reading either. She'd been in love with . . . what was his name? It would be too awkward to ask now, with the subject so obviously closed. But Aunt Meg *had* a tragic love affair! It was really most romantic. And terribly sad. I'd try to get details from someone else. It wasn't that I wanted to wallow in Aunt Meg's past, but I had an awful itch to know more of the details.

Poor Aunt Meg! I tried to picture her as a young, high-spirited college girl (in contrast to my quiet, reserved mother). I wished I could see a photo of her and the others from that time. And him . . . whatever his name was. Had he looked like Uncle Robert? There had to be snapshots around someplace. Either here or at Jess's. The only albums I'd seen were recent ones.

I must have been staring, trying to picture Aunt Meg

with longer hair. . . . Wouldn't she have worn it long? . . . instead of the brisk, swingy cut of today.

She looked up. "Yes?"

"Oh . . . I was just wondering. Would it be all right if I went in and mixed up a pair of gin collins drinks . . . without the gin, of course?"

"I think that is a truly marvelous idea," she said. "Go to it." And as I got up to leave, "Lindsay? I think I could handle a splash of gin in mine."

Obviously, I decided, putting together the ingredients, she's still shaky when it comes to talking about *him*. Well, I wouldn't poke around, dredging up sad memories. Not with her. I'd try to find out from someone else instead.

Chapter Twelve

Wondering about Aunt Meg's tragic love affair made me think of Rajee all the more.

He loved me. I knew he did. I could remember the look of fascination on his face when I'd say or do something on the wild side, like wading in an ornamental pool and striking a pose like Vishnu. When Jess would try to tone me down, Rajee would say in his protective manner, "No, let Lindsay alone. She is adorable."

Sometimes Jess would say to me afterward, "You ought to watch it a bit. You go too far sometimes."

"Oh, Jess, I do believe you're jealous that Rajee finds me so intriguing."

"That can change. He might not care for all that intrigue on a day-to-day basis."

I clearly remember Jess saying that, and my laughing in return. I was so sure then, of Rajee and of myself.

Sometimes when I was brushing Claudine's hair (she was like a cat that loved to be stroked) I'd talk to her about Rajee. I never knew how she'd react, though. She could lazily agree that he was certainly handsome, well mannered, well educated. Or she could purr, "Ah, Rajee, so much the frightened lover" (she'd pronounce it, *lovair*). "So much afraid of your big, wicked Papa, no?"

And I'd retort, "Why wouldn't Rajee feel timid? Father

acts as though he's some Mughal from the hills, swooping down to rape and pillage. . . ."

"Oooooh, my little one . . . so much in love, yet so helpless."

"I am not your little one!" I shouted the last time, stomping from the room and hearing Claudine's laughter trailing after me.

I knew very well Aunt Meg wouldn't make sport of me if I confided in her. But what good would it do? Either she knew nothing about Rajee, other than what I'd told her, or else she couldn't say because of Father.

I pretended not to, but I still noticed those studying looks she gave me from time to time. Another strange thing was the way she'd reach out to touch me, but catch herself and clasp her hands instead.

More and more I doubted that Rajee was the reason I'd been sent here. I decided it was much more likely that I'd been packed off because of Father and Claudine. Mostly that was because Meg looked worried every time I mentioned their separation or their making up. Anything about the two of them, in fact. Was she afraid they were doing so well without me that they were thinking of leaving me here on a permanent basis? Was I more than she'd bargained for?

I'd been behaving remarkably well, though. I hadn't thrown any of my famous fits, partly because there was nothing to get riled about. Also, I'd have felt a bit of an ass, acting up when Meg was so agreeable. I did rather wish, though, that now and then she'd tell me what was on her mind.

Really, there was nothing to say and nothing to do . . . about anything . . . until Father arrived. Then I'd insist on being let in on the events that concerned me. In the meantime I might as well find a job and earn a bit of money. It never hurt to have cash on hand.

After a couple of weeks of casting about, though I realized that what Hope had said was the unvarnished truth. There weren't any jobs to be had. I decided to go over to Jess's house and ask if there was a chance for me at the car wash.

"You must be out of your mind," was the not-very-kind response I got from him.

"I've seen girls work there," I retorted. "Doesn't one quit now and then?"

"Sure, but there's a waiting list. Besides, you'd fold at the car wash in a day."

"Exactly what does that mean?"

"It means you've never done any physical labor in your entire life."

"Then there's no time like the present to start, eh what?"

Jess gave me a long look and picked up a bunch of grapes from a fruit bowl. "Tell Mom I won't be home for dinner. I'll just be back to change, then I'm going out."

"With Hope?" I hadn't seen much of her lately. "How does she like her restaurant job by now? Does she still say working there makes her hair smell like soy sauce?"

"No, she's off that kick. Oh, here's Mom."

Jess gave her the message about missing dinner and left.

"Lindsay, how are you?" Aunt Janice asked, setting down a bag of groceries on the counter. "How are things going?"

"Fine. Here, let me help." I stuck some things in the cupboard. "Do you know the same company that makes this cereal makes the dog food that Aunt Meg advertises on her show?"

"I hope not from the same basic ingredients." She put ice cream into the freezer. "I haven't caught those commercials. Meg said they were clever. I really don't hear her show, though, unless I happen to be driving somewhere when it's on. How I get so involved in things is beyond me."

Aunt Janice folded up the grocery bag. "How did that cheesecake turn out that you were going to make?"

"Not too good. A bit soggy. But Aunt Meg said it tasted fine and Eliot made a pig of himself over it, so . . ."

"Eliot's fun, isn't he? Rather like an overgrown boy. But then, he has his serious side too."

"Do you think Aunt Meg will marry him?"

There was a slight pause while Aunt Janice ran water over the chicken in the sink. "Marry him? I don't know."

"It seems strange that she's never married in all these years," I said, trying to sound offhand, although I could feel my pulse quickening. "She's so smart and smart-looking. I mean, the kind most men would want to latch onto straightaway."

"Ummm. But when that one marriage didn't work out . . ."

"Didn't work out?"

Aunt Janice tore off a couple of sheets of paper towel to drain the chicken. "Maybe no one ever mentioned the fact that Meg was married for a time. It ended in divorce, though."

"Really? When was this?"

"Five, six years ago." She pulled out a recipe book. "We were in Bangkok then. We never did get to meet him."

Now it sank in. I'd forgotten all about that brief marriage. But here was a good chance to find out about her other love . . . if I was careful. I sat at the table and pretended to look through a bunch of cents-off coupons lying there. "Perhaps she just couldn't get over her tragic romance. When she was still in college. And in love with Uncle Robert's brother."

"Brian?" I could almost feel Aunt Janice looking at me.

"Yes." So that was his name. "I heard she really loved Brian. It was a shame he had to die that way."

"Ummm. Lindsay, would you see if there's any pineapple in that cupboard over there? I feel in the mood to make Hawaiian chicken."

She was also in the mood *not* to talk about Brian anymore. I hung around for a while, pretending to take an interest in the many wonderful ways to cook chicken, and then excused myself, saying there was something at home I needed to do.

I didn't need to do it, actually. The idea had just hit. The box in Aunt Meg's closet, the one I had seen the first day, could very well hold items of interest concerning the mysterious story of Brian. Perhaps it wasn't sealed *really* shut. Perhaps . . .

I went back to the house. Meg wasn't home yet, though she had said she might be early. I went into her room. It seemed to be witnessing my intrusion, silently chiding me.

Inside the closet I saw an empty space where it had been. The box was gone! Had Aunt Meg suspected?

I could feel my face flaming, as though I'd been discovered. Or as though she'd *known*. I started out . . . and there, on the other side of the closet, shoved among some luggage, there it was. The tape had been loosened. I could easily, without anyone knowing . . .

I hesitated. And looked at the box, just sitting there, waiting. And then I walked out. I could almost hear my father saying, "Decent people don't do such things." I was decent, after all. Curious as anything, but basically decent. Thank goodness I was. Just as I got out to the hall I heard Aunt Meg's car door slam.

I don't know why . . . maybe because I had a slight case of the guilts . . . but I chatted almost nonstop to Aunt Meg about her job during dinner and even asked when I could go to the studio with her.

She looked a bit surprised. "Any time, Lindsay. I told you that."

"I'm going out tonight, so maybe in a day or two when I can stand to lose the sleep?"

She laughed. "Getting up at seven isn't exactly daybreak, Lindsay."

As I started to help with the dishes she said, "I'll do it. Go get ready for your date."

"It's not a date. I'm just going to an outdoor concert with Turk, in the city."

"Make sure he drives carefully, Lin." She smiled. "I guess I sound like a nervous Nellie."

"No, more like a mother."

Aunt Meg dropped a plate. It smashed into at least six pieces.

"I'm sorry," I said, stooping to help pick them up. "I didn't mean to imply . . ."

"It's nothing. I lost my grip, that's all."

Still and all, what I said must have shook her up. She even looked a bit teary-eyed as she said, "Good-bye."

I wondered, after I left, if she dashed to the nearest mirror to look for wrinkles and the odd gray hair. Really. She might not be *old*, but she wasn't a kid either. Grownups could be so touchy sometimes.

In a couple of days I did go down to the studio with

Aunt Meg. On the drive she said, "Let me warn you about Murray. He likes to kid around. Too much sometimes. But on the air my partner's a real pro."

"Is he married?"

"Is he ever. Seven kids. There's the building, up ahead on the right."

As we swung into the lot, Aunt Meg put a white card into a slot and a barrier gate went up. We parked, walked into the building and rode up to the top floor. We went into the newsroom where teletype machines were spewing out news copy and typewriters were clicking away.

To the people milling about, Meg said, "Donna, John, Greg, Marilyn, this is Lindsay. Come to watch the stars at work."

They all said hi and chatted a bit, and then the woman named Marilyn brought coffee for Meg and asked if I wanted a Pepsi. I told her thanks, maybe later.

"Lin, just make yourself comfortable while I go over the spots," Meg said. She got into conversation with a bearded guy. Since nothing made sense to me I didn't really listen. The place wasn't the super-swank kind of room I'd expected. It was rather cluttered, as a matter-of-fact, with desks and file cases and lots of shelves filled with books and papers.

After a while Murray came in, wearing a Chicago Cubs baseball cap. "Hello, fans," he said, "another double-header today? Bleachers stacked with adoring mobs?"

"Murray," Aunt Meg said, handing him a sheet of paper, "do you know anything about this copy change? Has it been okayed? I thought we were supposed to go with the standard for the rest of this week."

"Beats me. Hey, Kramer?" he bellowed. "Get yourself over here and explain things out." He noticed me. "And who is this? Don't tell me. You must be the romance writer, here for the big interview. Oh, Miss Desiree de Cleavage, I was deeply touched by your latest . . . *So Lusty My Heart.*"

"This is Lindsay," Aunt Meg said. "Here to observe."

"Aha! She is spy from rival network? Guards!"

"Murray, save it for air time, will you?" Aunt Meg said. "We've got a few things here to clear up."

He settled down and they checked commercials, features, and stuff, always with an eye on the clock. About two minutes before they were to go on the air, Aunt Meg motioned for me to follow her into the studio, where she and Murray settled into chairs in front of microphones at a U-shaped table. Nervously, I watched the hands of the big clock move. Meg and Murray seemed so casual and relaxed. Then with just a few seconds to go, they stopped talking, made a couple of last minute motions to each other and then on the dot, she said, "Good morning, this is Meg. . . ."

"And this is Murray . . . for the *Meg and Murray Show!* There was a bit of music and then Murray said, "First, the news headlines. . . ."

After that, Murray said, "And now, let's hear about how badly traffic is snarled up today. Joe, you up there in the whirlybird?"

The guy gave the traffic report then, from a helicopter. Murray switched off his mike, turned to me and said, "How'm I doin', Sunshine?"

I shrugged. "Fine, I guess." I didn't let on that I'd never actually heard this part of the show before.

"Mur . . ." Aunt Meg said, "I think we should work in the best produce buys before we throw it to Chris."

"Sounds good," Murray said.

They got back on the air then, and I have to say it became rather boring. Aunt Meg must have noticed because when they started into what they called a recorded feature she called Marilyn on the intercom and asked her to show me around.

"Ever been in a studio before?" Marilyn asked, when we got outside.

"No." I could hear Aunt Meg's voice coming through from somewhere.

"I used to work at a TV studio. It was more exciting but I lost my job because of . . . oh, well. Are you Meg's kid?"

"Kind of. Related. I live with her now."

"Want some breakfast? The commissary's two floors down."

"Splendid. I am starved, rather."

She left me with a Danish and milk after I assured her I could find my way back.

The rest of the show, with interviews and some kind of contest, went fairly fast. Meg and Murray seemed totally relaxed, as though they were friends who got together for a chat. Afterward, though, they were all business as they went over some material for the next day. Finally we left.

"So, Lindsay," Aunt Meg said as we walked down the hall, "now you've seen how I work. Today was an easy one."

"I think it's hard, actually. The work. But you make it seem easy."

"Well, aren't you nice?" She looped an arm around my shoulder.

Down in the lobby I saw a woman nudge her companion and say, "Don't look now, but that's Meg Collins. . . ."

"Ohhh, wait'll I tell Henry!"

Aunt Meg seemed not to hear.

We shopped, had lunch, and chatted about this and that. Every once in a while I'd find myself looking at Meg too hard. It was as though I'd found the working-woman side of her, and I already knew, of course, the relaxed at-home side of her. But the romantic, tragic side hadn't come into focus. Not yet. Well, staring at Meg wouldn't help. With the years, she had hidden that side of her safely away. Like the box. But boxes could be opened. At the right time. It was just a question of when.

Chapter Thirteen

July arrived. My father didn't.

"Business problems," Uncle Robert said. "Unexpected complications. You know how it is."

But Father had promised. I'd talked to him just a week ago on the telephone. "I promise I'll try," is what he actually said.

Jess and his dad were going downstate in a day or two to check out the corn growing operation. "Want to ride along, Lindsay?" Uncle Robert asked. "You may find it interesting, seeing farm country. You know, the States isn't just big cities and suburbs. There are lots of small towns, too, and farms, and ranches."

"I guess I'll go," I told Turk that evening during a TV commercial, "though I'd prefer to visit a ranch. We simply adored cowboys overseas and as children we'd go about imitating them. Ruthanne still does it at times, and looks rather an ass, I'd say. Don't you agree?"

"I really hadn't noticed," Turk said.

"Oh, you're so unsatisfactory," I told him, giving his arm a little punch. "You just don't gossip at all."

"I'm sorry," he said in a rather abject manner. "I guess I've never learned how."

"Learned how!" I had to laugh. "But Turk, anyone can be a gossip without the least bit of trying, you know. All that needs doing is to comment on people's strange little faults, annoying habits, and so on."

"I see. Well, if you think I should, I'll try to start noticing."

I looked at him, so solemn. "No, Turk, I guess you should stay the way you are. If you started picking up on everyone's faults, where would I be?"

He pushed his glasses back into place. "But do you have any faults? I've never noticed them."

Wow.

The TV thriller came on again. It had the basic looney skulking around, and some scary effects but I found I couldn't concentrate. I'd been feeling groggy lately because I hadn't been sleeping well. I even cried out sometimes, enough to awaken me and also Aunt Meg.

Just this morning she had looked at me with concern and asked, "Is something troubling you?"

"No. Why?"

"Lindsay, it might help to talk about it."

Slamming the cupboard door shut I'd said, "There's nothing wrong!" I hated my tone that made her cringe ever so slightly, but I was jumpy. I didn't know what was wrong. All I knew was some kind of threatening revelation seemed to be hovering about in my dreams, like the shadowy figure lurking on the TV screen. It wasn't a person, though; it was something else from which I had to protect myself.

"Shall I turn it off?"

I realized Turk was staring at me.

"No . . . why?"

"You're so tense. Look at your fists."

"I wish people would stop staring at me! I wish they'd just leave me alone!"

"I'm sorry." Turk looked like a fearful pup.

I patted his arm. "It's not you. Really. It's . . . I don't know what to say. It's like tension building up and you know something's going to happen, but there's nothing you can do, because you don't know what . . . or why."

"Maybe I should leave so you can get a good night's sleep."

"It's worse when I'm asleep."

That night I woke up, damp with perspiration, from the same sort of dream.

During the next morning the heavy feeling of dread still hovered. And then it happened, the explosion. It arrived with the afternoon mail.

The letter from Rajee was brief. It read:

> *My dear Lindsay:*
> *I feel quite desolee to be required to say this in a letter. The proper thing to do would be to tell you in person, but, of course, that is impossible in the circumstance of your being so far away.*
> *The fact is, I am engaged to be married. The young lady who so honors me is one I have known for some time, since we were children, in fact. But Pritam and her family moved to another city some years ago and most recently moved back and we have renewed acquaintance. Both families are most joyous at this felicitous turn of events. As I hope you will be.*
> *May I expect your blessings and good wishes? For I know you are a most sweet and gentle soul who will rejoice in the good fortune which befell this guy at so recently a time. I await your answer with trembling anticipation.*
>
> *Your always good friend,*
> *Rajee*

116

For starters, I, the sweet and gentle soul, picked up the nearest object — my bedside clock — and flung it against the wall. When the alarm started wailing I picked up the thing and flung it down the hall, banged the door shut and kicked it. With my forearm I swept everything from my desk onto the floor, then stooped over, picked up his photograph, recently framed, cracked it to pieces on the metal wastebasket, and tore the photo itself into shreds.

Then the sobs came. And torrents of tears. Then my insides started heaving and I barely made it to the bathroom before losing my lunch.

I had subsided into some kind of stupor by the time Aunt Meg called to say she wouldn't be eating in that night. Assuming, from the sound of my voice, that she'd interrupted a nap, she apologized and then added that perhaps the country air would help my sleep patterns. Sure.

Later, I called Jess and told him the news with what I hoped was an air of detachment.

Jess gasped, though. "You've got to be kidding! You mean, he just wrote . . ."

"Exactly." Indignation took over. "He might at least have called."

"Too chicken." Jess cleared his throat. "What are you going to do?"

"Do? Jess, what can I do? It's all been arranged, don't you see? The parents . . . all these years? It was convenient for them, wasn't it, to have me around to distract Rajee until he was of marrying age . . . for someone else."

"Don't put yourself down like that, Lin. I'll bet, given the choice, Rajee would . . ."

"Oh, absolutely." I laughed hollowly. "Jess, you might

as well tell your family. But I don't want to discuss it. Okay?"

"Sure. You still want to go tomorrow, don't you?"

"Go where?" I'd forgotten all about the trip. "Oh. I might as well."

"Atta girl. I'll give you a wake-up call. Around seven. Bye."

Hanging up, I realized Jess had followed my cool and calm lead. But couldn't he see through it? Couldn't he tell that I needed him now? That I was on the verge of falling apart?

I walked around aimlessly, hearing Rajee's voice, seeing places we had seen together, reading in my mind his sweetest love poems. I thought I might be going out of my mind.

Slumping onto the sofa, I automatically flicked on the TV without turning up the sound, and stared unseeing at the images.

". . . thought you weren't here," I heard Meg say, coming into the room.

"Oh, you're home." I hadn't been aware of time passing.

She turned on a lamp. "Not so much traffic tonight. Good heavens, can you actually hear that? I must be getting old." She started to move on, then paused. "Has Eliot called?"

"No . . . I . . . I don't know."

"Oh, well, he will. Come talk to me while I change. Have you eaten?"

"Yes . . . no . . . uh . . ."

"There's plenty to choose from." Aunt Meg walked into her closet. I sat on the edge of her bed with a strange feeling of being there and yet observing myself being there.

"Which do you think," Aunt Meg said, coming out with two dresses, "for a business bash?"

"The . . . the . . . the . . ."

Aunt Meg put down the dresses and stepped toward me. "Lindsay, what is it?" There was mild alarm in her eyes. "What in the world is wrong?"

"Rajee . . . Rajee . . ."

"Yes, what about him? What's happened?"

I could only stare at her.

"He hasn't . . . ? Oh lord, he isn't . . . ?"

Dead? Did she think he was dead . . . that he had died like . . . like . . .

"Lindsay! Tell me."

"Rajee is getting married."

"Married?" She looked bewildered. "But isn't this rather sudden?"

Something about those words broke through my detachment and really grabbed me. "Yes, actually it *is* sudden. To me, that is, though not to the adults. How clever of all of you to conspire to get me away, so I wouldn't make a scene! Everything is suddenly so clear! You've all been going about, knowing, sharing whispers, but never letting on to Lindsay. Lindsay has to find out in the cruelest, coldest manner. . . ."

Meg tried to touch me but I flung myself away from her arms. "Leave me alone!"

"Lindsay, it's just not true. No one's been keeping secrets . . ." her voice faltered, "about Rajee."

"It doesn't matter! I don't really care! Good-bye, I may be gone when you get up tomorrow!"

"Lindsay! What are you saying?"

"Oh, never fear. I'm not about to throw myself before a speeding auto or even leave the country. You've all contrived to get me over here for who knows what reason, and you've made pretty damn sure I can't get back. Well, for your information, I don't want to go back, not now. For what? To dance at his wedding?" I could hear the hysteria rise in my own voice. "To watch Daniel and Claudine in their ghastly charade of fighting, drinking, and making up?"

I was crying hysterically now, and shouting. "The honest truth is there's no place for me now, not here or anywhere. You don't need me, they don't need me. . . . I'm just . . . just . . ." My voice broke and I fell on the bed, rocking back and forth and sobbing even worse than before, so full of despair that I couldn't have quieted even if I'd tried.

I heard the bell ring, and their voices, and felt Eliot's hands on my shoulders, telling me that it was all right, crying was all right, let it go. . . .

And then, finally, spent from the wracking sobs, I cried quietly while Aunt Meg cradled me in her arms and made soothing sounds, as to a little child. Eliot put cool cloths on my head, and hovered, not speaking.

This went on for some time. Eventually, limp and exhausted, I murmured that I was going to bed.

"I'll help you, Lindsay," Meg said. "You're like a little rag doll." She walked me to my room, helped me into my pajamas and then held me close, kissing the damp hair around my temples. "Baby, baby, if only . . ."

"Not now, Meg," Eliot said, appearing in the doorway. "Are you hungry, Raggedy Ann?"

"Not really."

"That means *possibly*. Possibly some scrambled eggs? Toast? Tea?"

"Ummm."

"I'll do it," Eliot said. "Stay with her, Meg."

I yawned from both physical and emotional exhaustion as I leaned back against the pillows. "You'd better get dressed for your party."

"Eliot called and canceled."

I didn't say anything, but I was glad they were sticking around.

When Eliot brought the food in on a tray I realized I was awfully hungry, and no wonder. I'd lost my lunch.

"At least now I won't have to eat breakfast before I leave in the morning," I said, breaking off a piece of toast.

"Leave?" Eliot said.

"Are you sure you're up to it?" Meg asked.

"I'll be okay." And to Eliot, "I'm going to visit a farm. With Uncle Robert and Jess. Part of the 'See America First' plan. Rather tardy in my case."

"See?" Eliot said to Meg. "The kid's okay. This one snaps right back."

"Don't let him get to you. Ignore him," Aunt Meg said with her pretend put-down smile.

I knew I'd feel bad again. I knew it would take a long time for the hurt to go away. But right now I was resting in a peaceful oasis. Meg and Eliot had that effect upon me for reasons I couldn't quite fathom.

Chapter Fourteen

The ringing telephone awakened me.

"You about ready?" Jess asked.

"Ready? It's only . . ." I looked, but my clock, of course, wasn't there. "What time is it, actually?"

"Eight. I overslept. Dad's about ready to go. Pick you up in ten minutes."

"Oh, please!" As it happened it took them longer but I still wasn't quite set to leave.

"Shouldn't you take along something dressier than shirt and jeans?" Aunt Meg asked, as I stood, bowl in hand, shoving down cereal.

Jess was jiggling with impatience. "Aunt Meg, we're only going to a farm and we'll be back tonight. If we ever get started."

"I'm ready, I'm ready." I kissed Meg lightly and started out. Then, not knowing why, I went back and put my arms around her. "I truly am sorry." I said into her hair.

"But you have nothing to be —"

"*Lind-say!*" Jess bellowed from outside.

I groaned, said, "Bye," and hauled myself out to the car.

Uncle Rob — who knew about Rajee if Jess had followed through — asked if I wanted to sit in front.

I told him I'd rather stretch out in the back because I wasn't much of a break-of-dawn person. He laughed and looked at his watch.

"How long will the drive take?" I asked as we got going.

"Close to three hours."

I made a little moan and looked about. There was no pillow so I made do with an old stuffed rabbit that Ruth-anne, great girl that she was, still kept about. "Wake me when we get there," I said.

I couldn't sleep, though. I'd hear the talk of Jess and his father and then stray thoughts of my own would weave into the tapestry of my mind. The sudden blare and whoosh of a big truck passing jolted me from the half-sleep.

I yawned. "Are we almost there?"

Jess turned. "We're not even on the interstate yet. Go back to sleep. I'll wake you when we see a moo-moo."

"Just wake me for lunch."

"Sure."

I knew I was being the soft and lazy lump Jess had had in mind when I'd brought up the idea of working in the car wash, but why be strong and alert now, when it served no purpose?

I punched the rabbit back into position and stretched out again. My mind clouded over and the real world began to recede. There was something going on in my subconscious, something wanting to get out into the daylight and be examined. But it was elusive. Rajee . . . Father . . . Claudine . . . Meg . . . *The Scarlet Letter* . . . the lily-white . . . the lily-white what? It hid. It wouldn't come out. But why did it trick me so? I was so weary. I wanted to sleep here, now, and at night. Peaceful sleep, with no fear, no dread.

"Dad, there it is, the turnoff!" Jess's voice brought me back.

"I see it."

I felt the car turn. "Are we almost there?"

"We're just on the interstate now," Jess said.

I sat up and looked out the window. The land was really flat. We drove on and gradually the commercial buildings and hubbub were left behind. On both sides of the road, as far as we could see, were fields of green growing things.

"Are those cornfields, then?" I asked.

"Soybeans," Uncle Robert said. "One of the main crops these days. Why don't we roll down the windows and get some real country air? You don't mind, Lindsay, if your hair blows a little?"

"Not at all." I folded my arms on their backrest and leaned my chin on them. "It's really nice . . . the sun, the warm breeze, the wheat in the fields moving almost like waves."

"You're probably thinking of that line in *America the Beautiful* . . . 'for spacious skies, for amber waves of grain,'" Jess said.

"Mmmmm. But mostly, I'm wondering if the corn will be as high as an elephant's eye, like in *Oklahoma!*"

Uncle Robert laughed. "It's funny and amazing to think you've seen an elephant before you've seen an American cornfield. I'm with you on one thing, though. I've never seen hybrid corn."

"You know what that is?" Jess said, turning toward me.

"No." I wasn't exactly perishing to hear either.

"It's corn that's been scientifically bred."

Fancy, I thought. "Oh?" I said.

"The test farms keep mixing strains of corn to come up with a kind that will yield more bushels to the acre. Right, Dad?"

"Bigger yield is one thing. They also try for kinds that are fast-growing and disease-resistant, that sort of thing."

Uncle Robert's look caught mine in the mirror. "Farmers used to save out big, well-formed ears for seed. Now they buy hybrid to up their chances of getting a better crop."

"Yes, but do they always? I mean, in India sometimes there's no rain and sometimes there's too much."

"It's the same thing here. Farming is always a prayerful proposition." Uncle Rob slowed a bit. "There's a pit stop up ahead. Want to break for coffee?"

Jess and I both said sure.

While I was finishing off the last of my sweet roll Uncle Rob wandered off for a bit.

"What did he say when you told him about Rajee?" I asked Jess.

"Not a lot."

"Probably *good riddance*. I imagine the adults think Rajee was just having me on." At Jess's silence I said, "Do you think that too?"

"No, honestly, I don't. I'm sure he liked you . . . maybe even loved you . . . in his way."

"I know he did, Jess." I rubbed at a coffee ring on the table. "But he's still under the influence of his family. And all the traditions."

"Well, yes. And then you weren't there."

I wanted to say, And whose fault is that? But a lump had formed in my throat and I was afraid of crying once again.

We all went back to the car. Jess talked his dad into letting him drive the rest of the way.

Riding along, I felt quiet tears misting my eyes and drying from the breezes rushing into the car. The expression "crying her eyes out" was such a strange one. Tears . . . even excessive tears . . . surely couldn't dislodge the eyeballs. But, I idly wondered, could enough tears fade out the color from one's eyes? "How much farther?" I asked after a while.

Uncle Rob turned and smiled. "Not too far. We'll go to the feed store on the edge of the town first, and then we'll go check out a typical farm."

I leaned back and closed my eyes. The breeze felt good. In spite of everything I was feeling a certain peace out here with growing things, and the blue sky above, and the road streaming ahead.

When we reached the little farming town we headed for the feed store. Some of the men wore business suits but most wore jeans and blue work shirts with patches that said *Prairie Seed Company, Inc.* Jess and I hung about but the talk of such things as ear retention and root systems, got pretty dull after a while. We went out to the Pepsi machine and then sat on the grass outside, drinking and talking.

"Okay, kids," Uncle Robert said as he came out. "We're going to take a run over to a farm." One of the guys from the feed store was with him.

"These your younguns?" he asked.

"Yes, sir." Uncle Robert looked proud. "This is my son, Jess, and Lindsay is kind of a shirttail relation." His tone was a bit lazy, as though he'd absorbed a touch of the country.

"Well, I'm sure glad to make your acquaintance," the man said, shaking hands as we got up. "Name's Bert Yeazel. This your first trip down this way?"

"Yes, sir, it is," Jess said.

The man turned to Uncle Robert. "We're into detasseling now. Think we should put them to work?" He laughed as though it were some huge joke.

"Not a bad idea," Uncle Robert said, all amiability.

"What's detasseling?" I asked, holding my blowing hair away from my face as we drove. "Is it anything like deflowering?"

Uncle Robert explained, but it was so technical I didn't get it. Anyway, the air and sun were making me sleepy.

We left the two-lane highway and drove over a black-topped country road and then finally up a lane to a farmhouse. Two dogs came out, barking their heads off. We heard a woman's voice when we stopped, and then the screen door slammed and a little tow-headed kid ran out and yelled, "Jaspar! Jeepers! Stop that yappin'! Go on, now!" The dogs, with one last bark, turned and trotted back to the shade of the house.

A woman, wearing a print top and dark slacks, came through the door. She was big-sized, but not fat. And she had a really great welcoming smile. "You must be the ones Arvin was talkin' about. Well, come on into the house."

As we got out of the car the dogs got up and gave a few on-duty barks but the boy raised a hand to threaten them and they slunk back to the shade.

The man, Mr. Yeazel, introduced us.

"Just call me Verna," the woman said. "And this here's our boy, Arvin Junior." With a fond smile she said, "He's our last youngun here at home. All the rest have grown up and gone off. Looks like Junior here came along just to keep us company. Junior, you go off and get your daddy to come up to the house. Almost time for dinner anyway."

"Sure. Can I take the truck?"

"Looks like you better. He's off in the west eighty, can't take the bike there, ruts are too big, and I don't want you gettin' hurt."

The kid, barefooted and skinny, raced over to a pickup truck sitting near a farm building.

"He's going to drive . . . that?" I couldn't believe it.

"Shoot, nothin' to it, now that he's startin' to get his growth," the woman said. "Makes him real proud. Last year his feet couldn't hardly reach the pedals, and he coaxed and begged, but his daddy said, 'No, son, I can't let you do it, not 'till you've grown some.'" She turned. "Well, come on into the house. No use standin' here in the sun."

I guess on a farm like this they could just leave keys in the ignition, because the kid started up the truck, arched it around, and took off in a cloud of dust. The truck disappeared down a dirt path toward the fields behind the barn.

When the farmer came back with Junior we sat around drinking iced tea for a while, and they insisted we stay for the noontime dinner. It was a huge meal of fried steak ("If I'd a known you were coming for sure I'd have fried up a couple of chickens too.") and lots of vegetables from their garden, plus still-warm apple pie.

Afterward, since the woman wouldn't hear of our helping with the 'washin up,' we went outside with Junior. He showed us the garden that he'd help plant and take care of, but the thing he was really proud of was his motorbike.

"Got it for my birthday," he said, straddling it and kicking up the stand. "Want to see me ride?"

"Sure."

He revved up the motor and took off down the drive toward the road, his shirt billowing in the breeze and his sun-bleached hair flattening against his head.

"Good heavens," I gasped. "Look at that kid go. I can't believe he's only eleven." I stretched to catch glimpses of him, now out on the black-topped road. "I wonder if he'd let me ride it."

"Lindsay . . ."

"He's coming back. Wow, it looks like fun."

The men came out just as Junior wheeled into the drive and stopped near us.

"Say there, Arvin," his dad called. "You're ridin' without shoes again. Now, what did I tell you?"

"I didn't go far," the kid said, ducking his head.

"Don't matter. I'm goin' out with these two gentlemen to check out the hybrid. You stay around and keep these two young people company."

"Yes, Dad."

They started off, but then the farmer turned and said, "Don't forget son, later on I want you to get out there and walk those beans."

"Today?"

"It's gotta be done. Might just as well get to it."

"All right."

After they took off in the truck I asked Junior, "What in the world did he mean, 'walk the beans'?"

The kid looked at me as though I were simpleminded. "Walk the beans. Walk down the rows and yank out the weeds the cultivator didn't get."

"Oh." I turned to Jess and said, "What was it again, that Mr. Yeazel said we should do? *Something* the corn?"

The kid spoke up. "Reckon you mean detassel. Boy howdy, now that is something to do! Pay's real good. As soon as I age some . . ."

"What kind of pay? Like how much?" I asked.

"I'm not exactly sure, but it's good money. Want to take a ride on my bike?"

"Sure!" I leaped forward and got on it. As I balanced the bike with my feet the kid explained how to make it go, how to slow it down, and how to stop. "Nothin' to it, really," he said.

I took off in a series of jerks, with the bike doing crazy side-to-side curves. Then I managed to straighten it out just before swerving onto the black-top. After a short distance I turned and brought it back. "Hey, hey, I made it!"

"You did real good," the kid said. He turned to Jess. "Okay, let's see you go."

Jess also got off to a shaky start, but managed to get the bike out and back without any spills. It was lucky for both of us that there weren't any cars on the road while we were riding.

"You did real good too," Junior said to Jess. "When you folks come back again, why you can take yourselves another ride."

"Boy howdy," I said. "I'll be back for sure."

We wandered into the yard and sat on old wooden benches. Jess and Junior began comparing their fold-up knives with all the extra tools. I tilted my head, closed my eyes and let the peace of the summer day take over.

I hadn't felt this tranquil for a long time. In fact, not since that time I'd run away in India and stayed at the *ashram*. It had been kind of filthy, though. Here, everything was fresh and clean and . . . wholesome. I wished I could stay. Not forever. Just until the sun and breeze and growing things drove all the hurt away and I was healed. And happy.

Chapter Fifteen

That afternoon we drove around with Mr. Yeazel, the feed store guy, to see lots of cornfields. In my view, when you've seen one, that does it for thrills. But according to this man every field he took us to was a different story in the saga of corn growing.

In one field we saw a bunch of kids off in the distance doing something. "There's a detasseling crew now," Mr. Yaezel said. "Hard at work. Man alive, it must be hot out there today."

"Can anyone get on a crew?" Jess asked.

"Sure, if they're big enough and don't mind hard work."

"Sounds good," Jess said.

"Say, son, if you want a job, why I bet they'd take you on. Always looking for new recruits, to replace the ones that drop in their tracks." He winked at Uncle Robert.

Jess bit his lips. "I'd like to give it a try. But how . . . I mean, Dad, are you going to stick around?"

"No, that's impossible. As it turns out, I will stay another day. But then I really have to get back."

"Oh, shucks, we could put him up somewhere," the farmer said. "Folks always have room for one more."

"Dad?"

"I don't know, Jess. I guess you could if you really want to. Might give you some idea of what . . ."

"Could I do it too?" I said the words almost without thinking. "I could use the money, for sure."

"Come on, Lindsay," Jess said. "It's hard labor."

"So? I'm not as weak as you keep implying."

"How old are you, sis?" the farmer asked.

"Sixteen. Almost seventeen."

"Why, shucks, you can do it then. We got lots of girls no more than fifteen, workin'. Some of them's better workers than the boys even."

"See? So could I stay, Uncle Robert?" Work, really hard work, I thought, might help me forget Rajee's letter and how it had hurt. "I don't think Aunt Meg would mind if I stayed here."

Uncle Robert shrugged. "If that's what you want. We'll call and see what she says."

"Well, then," the farmer said, "looks like we got ourselves a couple of good hands. Now, I'll just give ole Arvin Goebbert a call when we get back to the store and see if he can put the two of you up."

So it was settled. Later on, Uncle Robert checked into a Holiday Inn and called Aunt Meg to get her okay about my staying. That settled, Jess and I went back to the farm.

"You folks are sure the lucky ones," Arvin Junior said. "You're gonna be just rollin' in money."

Mrs. Goebbert actually seemed pleased to have us. "It sure will be nice to have youngsters around again. I miss my grown-up kids. And I can see Arvin Junior is pleased as punch to have company."

She even took me upstairs to a room that had been two of her girls' and fitted me out with some extra shirts. "You're going to have to change every day," she said. "You work up a real sweat out there. But girl, I don't know what you'll do about fresh underwear."

"I'll just wash it out every night," I said.

"And a toothbrush." Mrs. Goebbert brightened. "Why I believe we still have some new ones in the medicine cabinet. Seems like you never know when you'll need one."

That evening wasn't exactly the way I'd imagined it would be. There was no screened-in porch with a swing, no lemonade or games in the yard. Instead, we stayed inside where it was air-conditioned, drank 7-Up, and played Atari.

At about ten o'clock, the three of us were almost even in scores when Junior's dad came into the room. He had on his overalls and a pajama jacket. His face and neck were baked to almost a brick color, but at the V between where his work shirt ended and the pajama top began the skin was deathly white.

"Don't you kids think you should turn in?" he asked. "Got a busy day tomorrow. That is, if you're still game for the detasseling."

"Sure, we're game," I said, my eyes on the screen. "What time shall we get up?"

"I reckon about five, five-thirty."

"Okay." Then it sank in. "Did you say *five-thirty*? A.M.?"

"Yes, ma'am, I sure did." He turned to Junior. "Son, you'd best be gettin' to bed too."

"But . . . but . . ." I simply couldn't believe what I'd heard. "Five-thirty? Isn't it . . . well, dark then?"

"It won't be by the time you check in for work around seven. And by the time you get out to the fields that old sun will be gettin' up hot for sure. You kids got hats?"

"No," Jess said.

Mr. Goebbert shook his head, smiling. "I'll lay out a couple for you. Good-night, now."

After he'd gone and we were starting for the stairs, Jess said, "I didn't bring an alarm. Who'll wake us up?"

"My mom will, or I will," Junior said. "Pa says I can go along the first day, seein's you're here, but he said not to go coaxin' to work because it just won't be no use. I'm too young."

It seemed I had just closed my eyes when Junior came in and nudged me. "Time to get up."

I moaned. I heard Jess moan from the next room.

Downstairs, breakfast was all ready. I looked at the eggs, toast, cereal, bacon, and ham and felt a bit sick. "I never eat much this early," I said.

"You've never in your life been up this early," Jess commented. "Come to think of it, neither have I."

After a bit of urging ("It's a long time 'til lunch") I finally managed to swallow a piece of toast and black coffee. Jess, trying to act the farmer, ate like one.

"Now here's your lunch," Mrs. Goebbert said, handing us paper bags. "And Arvin Junior will take along this cooler with the soft drinks. Oh, and here's those hats. Better take them along," she said, handing each of us a billed cap with the Prairie Seed Company patch on the front.

Her husband drove us to the seed company building, and saying he'd pick us up at four, took off again. As the three of us walked across the lot, we were looked at, without much interest, by kids around our age or maybe younger. They were mostly just sitting along the curb, yawning.

"Hey, Peewee," a freckle-faced kid in a baseball hat called out, "what *you* doin' here, Short Stuff?"

Arvin Junior grinned. "Why, Alan, I come along to keep a watch on you. Heard you was goofin' off some."

The kid laughed.

"You'd best go in and sign up," Junior told us. "Then they'll tell you what crew you're on. Just pray to heaven they don't put you on no crew with that Pete Maurer as the head. He'd as soon spit in your eye as look at you."

When we came back out bunches of kids were milling around, with more being dropped off by the minute.

"All right, now," a young woman with blond Orphan Annie curls shouted. "I want everyone on crew number six to come over here."

I looked at Jess. "That's us. Could *she* be the crew leader? She's no older than I am."

The girl, Kim was her name, called out the names on the list and checked us off. "All right, let's get goin'," she said. She smiled, seeing Arvin. "Hey, Peanut, what you doin' here?"

"I just come along for the pleasure of watchin'," he said, while everyone laughed.

Both Jess and I kind of gulped when Kim told us to get into the back of the truck and she swung up to the driver's seat. "That little girl is driving this truck?" I gasped. "Oh, I don't know about this."

"Shucks," Junior said. "She got her license for truck drivin' way last year. Besides, she's oldern' she looks. Why, Kim must be gettin' onto nineteen by now."

It wasn't until later that we learned the reason for corn detasseling. That morning, Kim just hauled the truck up by the side of a cornfield and as the kids jumped out of the truck, she directed each to a certain row.

"Now, listen, guys," she said, scowling. "Yesterday,

when I went through the rows checkin', I found too many tassels. I don't want to find any today. So I'm tellin' you just once more, shape up or you can just forget about comin' back!" Her voice had a little twang.

The kids scattered. Kim turned to look at Jess and me. "Well?"

I swallowed. "We don't know what to do."

"What to *do*?" She stared at us as though we were a bit demented. "You just go up and down the rows and look for tassels."

I cleared my throat. "We've never been on a farm before. We . . . well, what's a tassel?"

Her eyes, a brilliant blue, widened. "I don't believe this. You're pulling my leg."

"Aw, Kim," Arvin piped up, "they're city folks. Want me to show 'em what to do?"

Without a word, Kim strode out to the nearest row of corn, with us following. "See this? This is a cornstalk," she said.

Neither of us said a word.

"See this?" She pointed to a plumed thing growing at the top. "This is a tassel."

"And we take it off," I said, a shade snappishly.

"Most of them have been taken off already by the machines. But sometimes they miss. So you're going to go down the row and pull off the ones it missed. You'd better *not* miss. We're goin' to have those inspectors from the seed company comin' through later and if they find more'n about one percent, we're in trouble. Got that?"

"Sure," Jess said. I could tell he was embarrassed.

"All right then, go to it. Hey, punk, where you goin'?"

Junior grinned. "I'll just go along for a spell and keep 'em company."

136

"Well, don't do too much yakkin' or I'll set you up for a scarecrow."

"Bossy little number," I mumbled as we trundled off to the rows Kim had indicated.

We walked along for quite a while without seeing what looked like a tassel. I was getting a bit uneasy, afraid we'd slipped up somehow, when Jess gave a shout. "I think I've found one!"

"That's a sure enough tassel," Junior said. "Yank it off."

"It's wet!" Jess said, pulling back.

We kept plodding along, finding a tassel here and there, and getting warmer by the minute. The sun was beating down on our bare heads and it wasn't even nine o'clock yet.

"Doesn't this row ever end?" I complained, wiping my cheek on my sleeve. "I can't see the end of it."

"It'll be comin' up in another hour or so," Junior said.

"Hour!"

"Well, I don't know. Maybe less. But then you got to move over to the next row and work your way back."

Remembering Jess's various remarks about my being a stranger to physical labor, I tried not to complain about my aching arms and gritty feet but I did rave on a bit about the heat. It was as hot as India — even hotter.

"Want me to run back and fetch you a cold drink if Kim's not lookin'?" Junior asked.

"No, thanks," I said, "I'll just carry on until I drop, like Gunga Din."

It was about ten-thirty when we got back to the starting point. We practically dragged ourselves up to the truck where the other kids were frisking about, enjoying their break. Junior produced Frescas from the cooler.

I held the chilled can to my cheek. "I'm burning up."

"You ought to of worn a hat," some kid said.

"Tell me about it," I snapped. So I'd forgotten, and left it in the truck. Big deal. So had Jess. I sat down in a bit of shade. To the kids I said, "Do you know *why* we're doing all this?"

"For the money, I am."

"No, I mean," I waved weakly toward the corn. "Oh well, never mind. It won't make a bit of difference when I'm dead, which will probably be in another hour or so."

When lunchtime finally arrived, a lot of the kids were still full of energy, chasing and wrestling and generally goofing around, but by late afternoon, when we got back into the truck, even the liveliest had toned down. It was *hot*. The hats we'd worn in the afternoon kept us from getting more sunburn, but now our hair was matted with sweat. My shirt was sticking to me. For the first time in my entire life I could smell my own sweat.

"I have never ever, in my entire life," I said, my voice bouncing as we rattled along in the back of the truck, "spent such a miserable day." Even in India, I thought, we had the sense to stay out of the main heat of the day.

"Aren't you comin' back, then?" a ruddy girl in bib overalls inquired.

"I might, if I'm still able to move," I said.

"Hell, at the rate we're gettin' an hour, I'd show up even if I was to be in a wheelchair," one of the kids said. "I sure do like the looks of that paycheck. Last year I bought me a CB to put in the old Chevy. It worked real good, but the Chevy broke down and now my dad's taken the CB and put it in the truck. Won't even let me drive it, though."

"So this year you aimin' to get you a Lincoln to put that CB in?" a kid asked. He got a playful punch.

When we reached the feed store, Arvin Junior's dad was

there to take us back to the farm. "Well," he said, as we drove, "how did the detasseling go?"

"Not bad, really," I said.

"Yeh, not bad," Jess said.

"It's better'n last year, though, isn't it, Dad?" Junior said. "Remember how it rained? Boy howdy, I thought they were all going to get drowned like rats out there in that field."

"You don't really mean to say they work in the rain, do you?" I asked, somewhat aghast.

"Girl, you work through sun, rain, hail or whatever is thrown at you. Detasseling just can't wait."

I wondered why, but didn't think I was up to hearing about it just then.

"By the way," Mr. Goebbert said, "your father called out at the farm today, Jess. He's comin' to fetch you after you've cleaned up some and says he wants to take you out to eat. Invited him there to the house, but he wouldn't hear of it."

For a while I toyed with the idea of going back with Uncle Robert. But after I showered and washed my hair I felt amazingly refreshed. I'd stick it out and show one and all . . . meaning Jess . . . of what stuff I was made. I wouldn't mind making a bit of money either. The biggest reason, though, was that I just wasn't ready to go back and deal with the reality of losing Rajee.

My alert feeling did a decided nose dive about halfway through dinner. I'd blink and try to focus on what Uncle Robert was saying but then my mind would go on vacation.

"I'll bet you didn't know that, did you, Lindsay?" he said when I was off on a mental break.

"Uh . . . what was that?"

"That every strand of corn silk is attached to a kernel of corn? And carries the pollen to it?"

"From the tassel," show-off Jesus added.

"Uh . . . oh, sure . . ." I yawned. "I knew that." I yawned again. My eyelids felt almost crusty. Was that where the old saying, *the sandman*, came from? Crusty eyelids?

"I just wish Daniel hadn't been delayed," Uncle Robert said. "When he does get here, I'll bring him right down, but he'll probably miss the detasseling."

"Poor Daddy," I said. My elbow, which had been propping up my weary head, gave way and I practically hit my chin on the table.

Uncle Robert laughed. "I may, at some time in my life, have had duller dinner companions, but I can't remember when. If you're sure, then, that you want to stick it out, I'll drop you off at the farm before I head back home."

I hardly remember the ride, or stumbling from the car, or falling into bed. I do remember, though, hearing Mrs. Goebbert say to Uncle Robert, "Now, just don't you worry. They'll be fine. We'll take good care of those two."

Sure, I thought, with a smile that turned into a yawn. Just like the witch took care of Hansel and Gretel. Another yawn. How good it felt to relax, to let drowsiness take hold. To slip peacefully into a night of dreamless sleep. I hadn't felt this good for ever so long.

Chapter Sixteen

In a way, the second morning was worse than the first because I already knew how awful it was going to be.

At the end of the day, though, I didn't have the totally weary feeling I'd expected. Not that I felt like capering on the village green, but I did have enough energy to get Mrs. Goebbert to take me to a store. I picked up a few essentials, like shampoo, sun-block cream, mint-flavored toothpaste, underpants, and socks. The crew socks I bought looked a bit bizarre with sandals, but at least they kept the dirt from grating between my toes.

Jess admitted that his muscles had been stiff and sore at first, too, even though he was in pretty good shape from work and from playing tennis a lot. Still, we could both do with a bit of resting up.

At the end of the week, I said to the girl sitting next to me in the truck, "TGIF."

"What? What's that supposed to mean?"

Hey. Here was something American I knew and she didn't. "It stands for *Thank God It's Friday*. There's even a restaurant up home by that name."

"What's so great about Friday?" she asked.

Good grief. Obviously, intelligence wasn't a requirement in this job. "If today's Friday," I said, as to a child, "tomorrow's Saturday." Still she looked puzzled.

"We get the day off . . . the weekend off!"

"Since when?"

"Since . . . what do you mean, 'since when'?"

"Ooooooh, girl, didn't you read the work sheet?"

"Work sheet? That thing they handed out? No, I didn't."

"Better read it, 'cause it lays it all out. If they require it, we gotta work right through the weekend. That's how it is."

"Slave drivers," I muttered.

I called Aunt Meg that night to ask if another letter had arrived. But what did I expect? An abject admission from Rajee that he'd made a terrible mistake? That I was, after all, his one and only love? Not likely. The betrothal was a fact. A fact that wasn't about to change.

"I'm sorry, Lindsay," Aunt Meg said. "No mail. But your father called. He now thinks he'll be able to come over in a week or so. Isn't that great?"

"I guess so. I mean, it really is . . ."

"What's the matter, Lindsay? Still feeling depressed?"

"A bit, now and then. But most of the time I'm too exhausted to feel anything. Wait until you see my hair. The sun's bringing out the red. And I'm peeling here and there and getting freckles on top of freckles."

"It sounds like a total farm experience."

"That's just what it is. What are you doing this weekend?"

"Eliot and I are going sailing with some friends. He's thinking of buying a boat himself. Do you know how to sail?"

"Not really. Not at all, in fact."

"Well then, we can learn together. It's hard work, I'm told, but fun."

"This is hard work down here, but not fun," I said.

"Lindsay, I'm a bit concerned. Would you want me to

drive down and get you? I'll be glad to, you know. We don't *have* to go sailing."

"No, no. It's not really *so* bad. I'm getting used to it. And the kids are fun, when we all get together."

"That's good. How long does this job last?"

"Just another week or so. Jess and I got a late start, missed the first week, but boy howdy, I'm just as glad."

Aunt Meg laughed. "You even *sound* like a farmhand. See you soon then, Lin."

It was kind of funny. To Aunt Meg now, I sounded like a farm girl. To the farm kids I sounded like a city girl. And to the city kids I sounded like a Brit.

But an even stranger thing had happened. I was a bit homesick. Only now it wasn't for India. It was for my suburban home. For my friends, Turk, Hope, and the others. But mostly it was for Aunt Meg. Somewhere along the line she had become the only person I could truly count on.

Days passed. Now that we were finally in the last stretch, the kids, like beasts heading for the stable, started getting frisky.

"If you guys are going to do any more horsin' around," Kim said late one afternoon, "do it now, and not in the truck. I don't want any accidents, not while I'm driving."

"All right!" A big kid named Milton pulled an ear of corn from his back pocket, tore off the silk, and shoved it down a girl's back. When she twisted around, he stuck it down her front.

The other girls jumped to the rescue, and that started off a wild bit of "horsing around."

Kim stood watching, arms folded. "I knew what they had in mind to do," she said to Jess and me, "when I saw them carrying that corn. So better now than later." She checked her watch. "We have to wait until the supervisor shows up anyway. Look at that Milton. He's like a big old dog."

"Kim, could I ask you something?" Jess said.

"Sure. Shoot." Her eyes were blue as cornflowers in the sunlight.

"Why do we detassel six rows and leave two? What's the reason?"

"Well, you know that corn pollinates itself, from the tassel?"

"Yeh, I know that much."

"Okay, with hybrid corn, we don't want the corn to reproduce its own kind. We want to mix in another breed to give a better yield. So the two rows left with their tassels on blow the pollen over to the rows with no tassels. That makes a new hybrid mix for seed corn."

"Now I get it," Jess said.

"What I told you just skims the surface," Kim said. "It's real scientific. Oh, here comes old Schaffer, finally."

She walked over and discussed something with the superintendent and took some papers. The kids, quieted down now, started getting into the truck.

After Mr. Schaffer took off, Kim motioned to a couple of stragglers to get into the truck and then motioned for Jess and me to come over. She asked if we wanted to ride up front with her. We did.

She had an REO Speedwagon tape going, but after a while she turned it down and said, "I'm kind of curious about why you guys are down here workin'. I mean, there's got to be easier ways of makin' money up in the city."

"There aren't that many jobs there," I said, and the money's usually just minimum. But I have to say this is a hard way to turn an honest dollar."

"Piece of cake from now on," Kim said, "Now that you're all broken in." She laughed.

"I'm glad to be involved," Jess said. "My father may want to get something like this going overseas and I wouldn't mind being a part of it. After college, I mean."

"But you're not going to be an ag major are you?"

"Ag? Oh, agriculture. No. More like biology, but I'm not really sure."

"I know how that is," Kim said, shifting gears at a stop sign just before the highway. "I messed around my freshman year, taking one thing and another, but now I'm going into farm finance. It's sort of a new field. I like it real well."

You never knew about people. Here she was, a girl as cute and trim as a cheerleader, driving a truck, bossing a crew, and headed for a career in farm finance. In her own way Kim was as different and full of surprises as anyone I'd met overseas.

The next day we awakened to a drizzly dawn. Arvin's dad had a gimmick that looked like a radio but which actually broadcast continuous weather reports. "Farmers live by the quirks of nature," he observed.

". . . developing into steady rain with a wind velocity of . . ."

"You were kidding, weren't you?" I asked. "The other day when you said we work whether it rains or not?"

"No, ma'am, I wasn't making a joke. That corn has got to get detasseled rain or shine."

"But . . ."

"You got any spare raincoats around here?" he asked his wife.

Finally we left, carrying lunches, coolers ("Seems like I ought to give you hot coffee instead of them Tabs."), windbreakers with hoods, and boots that nearly fit. They would be better than nothing, we were told.

Everyone was in a grumbly mood on the ride out and later the kids took their row assignments without enthusiasm. On that day when I gladly would have tramped the whole row without sighting a tassel, I found more than usual. Every time I reached to pull one I was showered from the leaves. Eventually the weather went from drizzle to steady rain. I wondered how Jess was faring. We'd been separated today.

Coming back, my jeans legs were soaked and my boots heavy with mud by the time I could see the truck on the road ahead.

Jess was already there, huddled against the truck with other kids. "I'm dying," I said, shivering. "Isn't there a law against all this? Exploitation of the young and innocent?"

"You can quit if you've a mind to," the kid named Milton said. "There's no one holding a gun to your head."

At about mid-afternoon the rain slacked off and the sun made a few halfhearted attempts to burn away the clouds.

We were a sorry-looking bunch riding back in the truck late that afternoon. Kids squeezed out water from the tail end of their T-shirts and tried dragging combs through matted hair. Some peeled off rainwear, which now was keeping in the cold. The kids closest to the open end of the truck began breaking off clumps of mud from their shoes and pitching them out to the pavement. Then the kids farther inside started pitching the stuff from their shoes, with lots of it accidentally creaming kids who were in the way.

By the time we got back to the feed store the truck was a mess and so were we. I was sitting there, trying to rub some mud off my shoulder, while kids, with wild hoops, jumped off the back end.

"Hey, Lindsay, get a move on," Jess called from outside the truck. "They're waiting for us." He started to walk toward the Goebberts' car.

"Wait a minute! Take the cooler!"

I handed it out to him and then remembered my windbreaker. "Just a second!"

"Well, come on!"

I was hurrying forward, bundling up the plastic jacket as I went, when suddenly my right foot hit a streak of mud. I had a second or two of wildly clutching at air before I landed on the pavement. Just before I passed out I heard the sickening sound of bone snapping.

When I came to — it must have been only minutes later — I saw faces peering down at me and heard all kinds of mixed commands, like "Lift her head," "Straighten out her leg!" "Don't move her, stupid!" "Call the paramedics!"

"I . . . I'm all right. . . ." I raised my head and then immediately fell back. "No! Don't!" I yelled as someone touched my leg.

I could feel sweat breaking out all over on me. I was biting my lips.

"Oh, Lindsay, does it hurt real bad?" Kim's face was near mine. "Now, just you take it easy. Help is on the way."

"Jess . . ."

"Here I am. Don't move, Lindsay. Oh, God."

The ambulance came and there was lots of commotion, with people offering up explanations as though they wanted to be a part of all this excitement.

"Just stand back, folks, please," the guys from the ambulance ordered. "Move back, please." One kneeled by me. "We're going to put you on the stretcher, honey. Just let us lift you. . . . Don't try to help. All right, easy, easy . . ."

The pain washed over me until I thought I'd scream, but I clenched my jaws. As they carried me, I tried to look around. "Jess?"

"I'm here," he said, stepping beside me. "Take it easy, Lin."

"Look now, what a brave little girl she is," I heard Mrs. Goebbert say. "Oh, I just wish I'd been there to catch her." And as they lifted me into the ambulance, "I'll follow right behind in the car. Now don't fret, honey, we'll look after you. Oh, Lord, the things that happen! And when you least expect it, seems like."

"Ma, I'm gonna ride along in the ambulance," I heard Arvin Junior say. "I've never been in one."

"No, young man, you're gonna come right along with me."

"Let him," I murmured.

In the end, he rode along with me and so did Kim and Jess.

"Now, miss, I'm going to give you a shot to ease the pain," the attendant said when we got rolling. "Just relax."

"Whoooeeee!" Arvin Junior said. "Would you just listen to that siren? I reckon every darn fool is gettin' out of the way!"

"Lindsay," Jess said, awkwardly patting my hand, "As soon as we get to the hospital I'll call Aunt Meg."

"Don't do that. She'll just worry. And what can she do?"

"I feel responsible," Kim said, from the other side of me. "I should have ridden herd on those kids more."

"It's nobody's fault," I murmured. "Just clumsiness." The shot was making me groggy, but at least the pain . . .

It came back, like fiery knives up my leg, as the paramedics moved me off the stretcher in the hospital and onto a different one. Then they left, talking to each other, and I realized that to them I was just part of their job.

Someone else was pushing me now, down the corridor, with my various friends tagging along. A nurse materialized. "This the Collins girl? Take her right to emergency. . . . The doctor is still here. . . . He'll be right down."

Someone else, a woman in regular clothes and wearing glasses, came trotting up. "Just a minute there, where are the parents? We can't admit her without parental consent. We need authorization, a signature."

"Well, my land," Mrs. Goebbert said, "I never heard of such a thing. Here's this little girl all hurt and Lord knows what and . . ."

"Are you a parent or guardian?" the woman asked.

"Well, looks like I am, right here and now."

"Then please step down to the office with me. And that little boy . . . bring him along. You should know children aren't . . ."

The voices drifted off. I could see the ceiling moving by as I was pushed down the corridor. "Jess?"

He caught up and walked alongside. "I'll stay, don't worry." Then, "I really do have to call Meg."

"Don't bother her."

"Bother!"

Kim came up beside Jess. "Lindsay, listen, you've got

to get through to a relative. I think it's against the law or something to treat kids without a parent's permission."

That started me crying. *I didn't have a parent!* I was alone here without any kind of relative and my leg was hurting a lot now.

"Just bear up a little longer, honey," someone said. "Lindsay? Is that your name? Here's Doctor Morgan."

The doctor was nice enough, asking questions, and touching my leg here and there and assuring me it would be all right. He had them take x-rays and then they put a cast on my leg, up to my knee. The pain pills they gave me helped some, but it still hurt a lot. I wouldn't let myself cry any more, though.

Next, they wheeled me into a room and lifted me onto the bed. "But do I have to stay here?" I asked. "I . . . I . . ." I felt lonely and afraid, that's how I felt.

"Just a day or two, until we check on any swelling, any complications. Now you just take it easy and rest. The nurse will give you a shot for pain and you'll be fine."

Sure I would.

Jess and Kim came into the room.

"I'm just warning you," I said. "The next person who tells me to relax and take things easy . . . !"

"I tried to reach Meg," Jess said. "She's not at the station or at home. I'll keep trying."

"Where's Mrs. Goebbert?"

"Out there, waiting. She wanted to be sure you're okay before she left. She'll have to drive Kim back to her car."

"Okay. I'm fine. Drowsy. Call me tonight, will you, Jess?"

"Call? I'm staying."

"You can't. Your clothes are damp." They'd taken mine

off and dressed me in a hospital gown before putting on the cast.

"I'm almost dried out. Anyway, I'm staying."

Kim left and Mrs. Goebbert came in and carried on for a while about what a little lamb I was, and then they all left. Except Jess.

I dozed for a while. They brought in a tray of food but I couldn't eat. I made Jess go to the cafeteria and while he was gone I dozed again. It must have been partly the pain pills. Part of it, though, I do believe, was just simple exhaustion from getting up so early so many mornings in a row. Well, so long to all that. I felt myself smiling and drifting . . . what a way . . . a way . . . to get to sleep . . . sleep late . . . in the morning. . . .

It was sometime in the night . . . it was dark . . . when I awakened to pain that shot up my leg and seemed to wash over me like a wave. It kept getting worse, wave after wave. I couldn't find the bell. "Oh . . . please . . . nurse . . . someone . . . please . . ."

I saw a shadow at the door. "Please . . . the pain . . . !"

The shadow moved into the room. It was Meg.

"Oh, baby, oh, darling . . ." She came to the bed and, stooping, put her face next to mine. "And I wasn't here." She rose slightly and rang the bell. "If she doesn't come right away . . ."

"She will." I took hold of her hand. "How did you find out? Jess?"

"He called just as we got home. We drove right down."

"We?"

"Eliot and I. He's out in the waiting room. He's almost as upset as I am."

"That's nice . . ." I winced from the persistent pain. "I mean, for him to . . ."

A nurse came bustling into the room. "You know, miss," she said to Meg, "it's 'way past visiting hours."

"I realize that," Meg said in a quiet tone. "But I just arrived. I . . . I'm family. I need to be with her. And right now she's experiencing a lot of pain. A lot."

"I see. All right. I'll get something." The nurse left.

"Is today Friday?" I asked Meg.

"No, Wednesday."

"Then you'll have to leave. Tonight." I hung onto her hand.

"No, I won't. Murray can carry the show. I've done it for him plenty of times. Every time his wife has a baby."

The nurse came back and turned on the light and gave me a shot. Aunt Meg looked pale and haggard. "Will this do it?" she asked, as the nurse rubbed the spot with a bit of gauze.

"She'll be out like a light. Listen, when you leave," she said to Meg, "put up the sides of the bed. We don't want her taking another tumble. Well, good night. Go to sleep, Lindsay."

"Go to sleep, Lindsay," I mocked in a low tone. "Take it easy, relax . . . that's all they keep saying around here."

"Sssssh." Aunt Meg turned off the light. "You really should, though . . . just let the medication take hold."

"Where will you be?"

"Right here. I won't leave. Close your eyes, darling. . . ."

Time must have passed. I was there, and yet I was somewhere else . . . somewhere else . . . and I couldn't see through the grayness. I was alone . . . and afraid . . . and something had happened. "Mommy! I'm hurt!" I cried.

From somewhere Mommy touched me.

But how could she touch me? I was alone . . . I couldn't see anything through the grayness pushing all around me . . . and I cried out, "I fell on the rocks and hurt my knee. . . . Where are you? I can't find you!"

And Mommy said, "It's all right, baby. Go to sleep."

I was in my bed then. "Tuck me in. Sing to me. But don't wake up Father. Stay with me. Promise?"

"I will. I'll stay."

"No . . ." I felt tears on my cheeks. "You say that, but when I wake up, you'll be gone. You're dead."

"No, Lindsay. I'm not dead." Mommy was crying, too, I could tell. "I'm here . . . to take care of you . . . always."

That's what she always said, but I knew better now. "No, Mommy, you'll be gone. You're dead. You're dead."

And the last sound I heard was Mommy sobbing.

Chapter Seventeen

When I woke up it was bright and sunny in the room. I looked at my watch. Holy petunia! Six o'clock and I had awakened without an alarm. I wondered what time they served breakfast in this place. I was ravenous.

With a bit of squirming I managed to reach and ring the bell. When the nurse came in I asked for something, anything, to stave off starvation until breakfast time.

"I'll see what I can do. How's the leg?"

"It doesn't hurt. Do I need to have these bars up? I feel like a caged creature."

"You do? Let's lower them then."

A dim sort of memory crept into my mind. "Was someone here . . . late last night? To stay with me?"

"Well, dear, I wouldn't know. I just came on duty." The nurse left the room to get my snack.

Meg. She had been here. I remembered talking to her and her telling me she and Eliot . . . but where were they now? I felt a strange little flutter in my chest. And later? Deep into the night? Had she been here still? No, it had been a dream. Only a dream. A dream come back after so many years. But I didn't want to remember.

"Well, look what we have here!" A young nurse's aide brought in a bouquet of mixed flowers. "Some people are mighty popular!"

"Who are they from?"

"Here's the card."

It said, "What a way to get out of work! Love from your detasseling friends."

I wondered if Jess had gone out to the fields, but shortly after breakfast he came strolling in. "Hey, klutz, how's it going?"

"Okay. How come you skipped work? You didn't need to."

"And let you lie around here gloating? No way. But seriously, how are you?"

"Jess, was Meg here last night?"

He looked at me strangely. "Don't you remember? Were you that knocked out?"

"Where is she now?"

"Eliot dragged her off around two or three A.M. to get some sleep. We all stayed at a motel. She must have been a wreck because I know Eliot was really concerned about her. I took his keys this morning, left a note, but I'd better get back. So, are you going to tell me or not? Does your leg still hurt?"

"I don't feel like dancing in the street, but it's not bad. Just kind of a dull throb. I'd like to go home."

"Hey, relax and play this for all it's worth," Jess said, smiling. "It's not every day a kid gets wounded in action. They may name a cornfield in your honor."

"I'd rather have a hybrid named after me. The *Lindsay Klutz Variety*. Could you suggest that?"

"At the next farm council meeting. Look, I really had better head back. They'll be wanting to come over." He touched my chin with his fist. "Keep up the spirits."

"Sure."

I was flicking the TV remote button from one channel to another when I heard Aunt Meg's voice out in the corridor, along with a man's. I realized it was the doctor's as he came into the room with Aunt Meg and Eliot.

"How's it going today?" he asked cheerfully, touching my toes. "Feel numb?"

"No." I smiled at Aunt Meg. "Hi. Oh, and Eliot . . ."

"Hey, champ," he said, coming to stand beside Meg. "You were really out for the count."

Aunt Meg's face looked pale, and there were little lines of, I guess, fatigue around her mouth. I couldn't see her eyes because she was wearing dark glasses. "Darling . . ." she said, touching my cheek, "are you really all right?"

"Sure." I took her hand and held it. "Could I go home?"

"Well . . ." She gave a quick look at the doctor. "I don't know. What do you think, doctor? Can she be moved?"

"Possibly." He was probing my leg just above the knee. "Any pain here?"

"No. Well, just a bit. I really feel okay though."

"Tell you what," the doctor said. "You relax and take it easy and we'll see. Maybe you can leave by this afternoon since there's no swelling."

When he left Eliot walked out with him. They seemed to be talking about cars, distance, and so on.

"Oh, Lindsay, I feel so terrible . . ." Meg bit her lips, "not to have been here sooner . . . like years ago." I had never seen her so trembly.

I felt vaguely nervous. "Don't worry," I said, trying to keep my voice level. "You're here now and that's all that matters. To me."

"Is it Lindsay? If things were only that simple . . ." As Eliot walked back into the room she broke into sobs. He raised her to her feet. "Now Meg, don't. This isn't doing any good. It's only upsetting . . ."

"I know. I'm sorry. Sorry." But the sobs continued and he led her out of the room, talking softly to her.

A sort of chill went over me. I'd never before seen Meg out of control. She wasn't the type. And judging by the dark glasses . . . she never wore them indoors . . . she must have been crying all night. About my leg? Hardly. It wasn't *that* devastating.

The dream. She'd been here during my dream. The dream that used to plague my childhood. But Meg had been part of it, last night. It was her voice that had said, "No, Lindsay, I'm not dead." I didn't want to think of it, to remember.

I pulled up the sheet and turned the TV back on and stared at the images on the screen. I didn't want to think about anything at all. I just wanted to go back to yesterday. To before. But I couldn't do that, could I?

By late afternoon, after more examinations and more conferences, it was decided I could go home. As they were getting me ready . . . Meg had bought a gown and robe for me . . . there was a knock on the door and practically the whole detasseling crew came swarming into the room, with a nurse yelling behind them.

"Hey, guys!" I shrieked. "Thanks for the flowers. Am I ever glad to see you! I'm leaving in a while."

"That's what we figured you might be fixin' to do," Marvin said. "But we weren't going to let you go without us puttin' our names on that cast. Right, gang?"

"Right!"

I introduced them to Meg and to Eliot, who seemed to

be getting a large charge out of it. "And this is Kim," I said, holding out my hand to her. "She's the section boss, and mean as a snake."

"No kidding," Eliot said, with that big, all-out smile of his. "You bossed around this bunch?"

"They didn't give me too much trouble," Kim said. "After I read out the riot act." She handed me an envelope. "Here. It's your pay. I figured you might be up and leaving. We sure will miss you, Lindsay. And Jess, too. Here's your pay, Jess."

"Great. Thanks."

Kim turned to Meg. "They're real good workers, even if they are city slickers." She leaned over and lightly kissed me. "Keep in touch, will you? And if you ever get a chance to come down again, why look us up."

"I will, Kim. And if you ever come up our way . . ." I'd never have thought I'd feel sad about leaving. "Will you tell the Goebberts good-bye for us? Oh, gee . . . Arvin Junior. I wish . . ."

The kids started signing my cast then, and one girl handed me a tassel. "This is a souvenir," she said, "of what you did and stuff."

"Thanks a lot. I'll stick it in a bud vase and keep it." I did, too.

I don't remember a lot about the ride back. Jess and Eliot sat in the front, and I lay in the back, my head on a pillow on Meg's lap. I was so medicated I dozed through the whole trip. At the house Eliot actually carried me in, though I must have weighed a ton, with the cast and all. He and Meg got me into bed. Later, I knew Aunt Janice came in, and Uncle Robert, who said something about regretting his part in all this. "Don't feel bad," I murmured, and then added something weird like I'd enjoyed every minute of it. He laughed.

I didn't see or hear Jess or Ruthanne. Once when I was dozing Aunt Meg roused me to give me pills, but then I tumbled back to sleep. For a while.

As from a distance I heard Aunt Janice suggest, "Shouldn't we close the door?" And Aunt Meg's soft, "No, what if she calls? Let's just go into my room. We can talk there and yet I can hear her if . . ."

I fought to keep awake. My muscles tensed up. I knew that what they were about to say was significant. Darn the cast. I couldn't move out of the bed, but I propped myself up on one elbow to strain toward the voices.

". . . think she knows?" Aunt Janice.

"I can't be sure. Aunt Meg's voice was soft, but still it carried. "Last night . . . oh, Janice . . ."

"It seems to me you were working up to it anyway," Uncle Robert said. "So perhaps . . ."

"But not like this. It was so . . . so *wrenching*. I wanted to do it in a more controlled way. I wanted to . . . to give myself a chance."

"Who knows? Maybe it's better this way," Uncle Robert said. "And if she takes it in stride, and Daniel agrees, there's no problem. At least you don't have to wonder for long. He'll be here in a day or two."

"How strong is the attachment, would you say?" Now it was Eliot's voice. A regular family council.

"Well . . . he raised the girl. From an infant. So naturally . . ."

"Of course." Eliot again. "But considering the difficulties with his wife . . ."

"Nice enough woman." Uncle Rob's voice. "Flighty, though. Without much idea of how to raise a teenager."

"But she's so young herself," Aunt Janice said. "It was as though they were girls together."

"Look, Meg, I think you should look on the bright side." Uncle Robert's voice was very clear now. "I have a feeling Lindsay will be overjoyed at . . . to find out. I honestly think she's been looking for guidance . . . direction . . . for a long time."

"Sssshhhh," someone said. And then the voices were lowered so that I could only make out a word here and there.

I leaned back on the pillow. What had they been saying? What was this all about? Deep down I thought I knew. But It didn't make any sense. I felt scared. My life was suddenly in a lot of pieces and none of them fit together. But Meg and Uncle Robert and the rest — they were all concerned. I wanted to call out to them, to say, "I heard! Tell me! Tell me what it all means!" I started trembling. And then I started to cry. I didn't know why. Only that I was lost and lonely and yet I couldn't reach out to the people I loved the most. Whatever it was, they didn't want me to know. Not yet.

My sleep that night was so troubled that I felt terrible in the morning. Meg, feeling my forehead, looked concerned. "Is there something wrong, Lindsay?"

I moved my head back and forth. "No."

"But . . . let me take your temperature." She did, and looked more worried. "I'm calling the doctor."

"No!"

"I must." Afterward she said, "It's for your own good."

I started to cry again. I couldn't help it.

She sat on the edge of the bed and cradled me in her arms. "Honey . . . what . . . ?"

"Is it . . ." I snuffled. "Is it also for my own good that you gave me away?" The words came out by themselves.

"My God!" I could actually feel her heart beating. You heard!"

"It's true, isn't it?" I still didn't know exactly what it was I was saying. "Tell me!"

"Oh, Lindsay, not like this! It shouldn't be like this!" She began sobbing so hard the bed shook. I started crying too.

"Don't Meg, please don't. Meg!"

She couldn't stop, though. With each breath, sounds came from deep in her throat and then she'd exhale in a series of catches that was really quite alarming.

"I'm sorry," I said, confused and frightened. "I'm sorry. Please stop. Please!"

She shook her head as though stopping now was impossible.

I held her tight, and as she gradually quieted down from the sobs I said, still crying, "I love you . . . whatever it is, it doesn't matter. I love you dearly." Another thing I didn't know I could say.

I handed her some tissues. She covered her face with them. "You probably won't," she choked out ". . . love me . . . when you hear." She was trembling now. "When you hear the real story."

"I have this feeling . . . that I already know. But tell me, please."

She took away the tissues, closed her eyes and swallowed. "It happened a long time ago."

"Before I was born?"

"Yes, Lindsay, before that."

I lay there, waiting.

She gave a final sniff and took a deep breath. "I was

in college. Young. Too young. But we were in love. That's the only thing that mattered. Being in love. We got married one weekend. Lied. I did, about my age."

I couldn't take my eyes from her.

"My parents, when they found out, had the marriage annulled. They sent me to a different college. Oh, Lindsay, I was really so young. I realize that now. But I thought of myself as quite mature, and quite sure that my life was over."

"What happened?" I was trembling now too.

"His life . . . Brian's . . . really was over soon after. He died in a skiing accident. He was Uncle Robert's brother."

"Yes, you told me that." But there was more.

"And then . . . and then . . . I discovered I was going to have his baby . . . Brian's. I thought I was going crazy . . . and yet in a way it was a comfort. But when you were born . . ."

Me. I knew it. I'd felt it. But it was too much . . . now . . . all at once. "Me . . . !"

Meg clutched me as I started shaking and sobbing too, partly out of fear at all these strange things being said. I wasn't *me.* I wasn't who I'd thought I was. My whole life was all in a jumble . . . a big mistake, with names and places and people . . .

"Please . . . please don't hate me." Meg's head was bent.

I smoothed her hair. "Meg, I don't hate you. I'm just so confused . . . and scared . . . like . . . like when I dream. I feel so lost."

"Of course, you must," she said in a muffled voice. "And to hear it this way . . . all of a sudden." She moved her head back and forth. "It wasn't . . . certainly wasn't the way I'd planned to tell you at all."

"When and how, then?"

She raised her head, swallowed and murmured, "I don't know. I kept thinking I'd wait for the right time . . . whenever that was . . . and tell you gently, gradually. But now!"

"Please tell me the rest of it. After I was born."

She looked beyond me. "In spite of my wanting to hang onto you, the only part of Brian that was left, they finally convinced me I shouldn't. Not at my age. A college girl with no way to raise you and so forth. And so . . ."

"Daniel. Your brother."

"He and Katherine couldn't have children. They were going overseas and would be there for years, so far as they knew. They wanted you, to raise as their own. It tore me apart, but I knew it was the best thing to do. For you. For them."

"Oh, Meg . . ." *Mother.* I couldn't quite say it. "And I never even guessed. I thought all this time my mother was . . ."

Meg's eyes misted again. "When Katherine died I wanted you back in the very worst way, but then you were all Daniel had. He loved you. As though you were his very own."

"Father! Oh no . . . he's *not* my *father!*"

She wiped the tears from my cheek. "He is in the true sense of the word, Lindsay. He loved you totally all those years. Knowing that made it easier for me and yet it was that very fact that kept me from . . . well, interfering, trying to keep in touch. I wouldn't let myself write to you, ever. As for visiting, it was out of the question."

All of these sudden revelations . . . new, real mother, no more real father . . . ! "I can't quite realize all this," I said. "I don't even know who I am!"

"I know this is all an awful shock to you. A cruel shock."

"Not cruel. It's just something that will take a bit of getting used to. I still can't quite believe it."

"I know. And here I am, helping you a lot by falling apart."

Without thinking, I said, "At least you're not on mike."

Meg laughed and shook her head.

"You've been under a lot of tension, I guess. All this time," I said. "While I've been happy-go-lucky ignorant." I listened. "Was that the doorbell?"

"Oh, good Lord. Who?" She grabbed more tissues and swiped at her cheeks. "Ruthanne? No, she'd come in at the back. It must be the doctor!" She squeezed my hand and left.

I heard sounds at the door and then the doctor saying, "Broke her leg, eh? Well, let's have a look." He appeared in the room. "Hello, there young lady. Feeling the worse for wear?"

"Not really."

The doctor's expression was a puzzled one as he looked from the sodden mass . . . Meg . . . to the equally sodden me. He checked my toes, my knee. "Still experiencing some pain, young lady?"

"No."

Now he looked really puzzled. "Let's check the temperature." He did that, took my pulse, and listened to my heart.

"Slight elevation of temperature," he told Meg. "But within the normal range, considering. Nothing to be alarmed about." He stood up, put the things back into his case and said to her, "If it will relieve your mind, we can take her in for x-rays, but I really can't see the need."

Meg moistened her lips. "I'm sorry I made it sound so

urgent. I was upset. We've gone through quite a bit, and then this morning when she seemed . . ."

"I understand." The doctor picked up his bag. "I'll phone in a prescription for a sedative." He eyed Meg. "I don't know who needs it more . . . mother or daughter."

Meg and I looked at each other at the same moment. *Mother or daughter!*

I heard the doctor out in the hall say, "Now, Mother, you shouldn't get so upset over a broken bone. With youngsters it's just a part of growing up."

Mother . . . again! I sat up, waiting for her to return. When she did, I held out my arms and she all but fell into them.

"He knew! Did you tell him?" I asked. "Does he know you?"

"No, he's covering for my regular doctor."

"It's so strange . . . some people knowing all along," I said. "Haven't you ever wanted to tell me the truth?"

"Have I ever! Sometimes I had to get up and leave the room, I ached so much to hold you and claim you."

"Why didn't you, then?"

"I didn't want to tie you up with my own feelings. I had to wait. To see if you could come to love me on your own."

"Well, I do. I really do. Quite honestly though, not at first. I guess I resented you, rather. I thought you were in on the plot to separate me from Rajee."

"To separate . . . ? But Lindsay, if that had been it Daniel could have sent you to a school, or better yet, a convent."

"I guess. Like they did with Claudine. I thought later it was Claudine, you know. Her being a bad influence on me and all." I frowned. "Was Father in favor of my coming here?"

"It broke his heart to think he might lose you. But he knew I wanted you desperately."

"Why now? After all these years?"

She winced. But I was feeling a bit of hurt myself.

"You'd become a dream image to me. A tiny baby, and then a child in a photo. Real and yet not real. And then they came back, Uncle Rob's family. Jess and Ruthanne chattered about you constantly . . . not knowing the facts."

"Did that make you sad?"

"Sad? More like crazy. I wanted to hear and yet it hurt to hear. It became an obsession with me. I had to see you. To get to know you."

"If someone had just *said*. If I'd known *why*. I couldn't understand why I was sent here."

"I didn't want you to know, to feel obliged to be decent even if you disliked me."

"Wow. And here I thought you were just doing Father a favor, getting me off his hands. That you and Eliot were just being good sports." After a moment I asked, "Are you going to marry Eliot?"

"Probably. If it's all right with you."

"Sure. I like him a lot. Does he know about me . . . who I am?"

"Yes, he does. And he likes you a lot too.

"Something else. When are we going to tell Jess and Ruthanne?"

"How about tonight? Can you hold off until then?"

"Only if I don't see them before."

"We'll invite the whole family for dinner," she said. "Really celebrate. Oh, Lindsay, you can't imagine how often I've pictured this taking place." She paused. "What are you thinking?"

"I'm remembering the dream. The one I had sometimes,

a lot lately. I was lost and crying for my mother. And to think it's you I've been looking for all these years. My own real mother!"

"Oh, Lindsay . . . my baby."

"Now I see why you looked at me in that puzzling way."

"You noticed? I was trying to see the toddler I'd missed, the ten-year-old, the young teenager. But I never could. It's like that story we both read . . . not being able to picture the past. But it's enough for me, having you as you are today. We'll start from here."

I don't know how it was possible, after so many tears, that we could cry again. But we did.

This time it felt good.

Chapter Eighteen

That afternoon Meg brought out the mystery box from her closet. Thank goodness I hadn't looked at it that day I was tempted because I don't know how I'd have handled seeing the things inside.

There were snapshots of me as an infant that I had never seen before. Then, familiar photos of me at monthly intervals. Then they became just birthday pictures, one from each year. I glanced up at Meg and caught a look of sadness before she remembered to smile.

"Do you have any pictures of . . . my father?"

"Here." She handed me a separate envelope.

The first was of a young man with a tennis racket, smiling into the camera. "He looks so young!" I couldn't imagine that this was my real father. "And he looks a little like Jess, around the eyes."

"I've noticed that. And certain expressions too. It was brutal the first time I noticed them. In some ways you and Jess resemble each other . . . it's from your grandmother."

"Sometimes kids thought we were brother and sister."

We went through the other photos and then Meg — Mother — unwrapped a piece of tissue. "Here's a little sweater you wore as a baby. And a cap." They were white, and so tiny.

"I actually wore these?"

"You did. They're the only things I kept when I let you . . . when . . . when you left with them."

"What's this?" I asked, trying to steer her away from the weeps. I could see, obviously, that it was a dried-up rose.

"It's . . . it's a flower I saved from Brian's . . ."

"Oh." What a wonderful steering away job I'd done. "Do you still think about him? A lot?"

She took a deep breath. "Lindsay, I'd like to say yes. The truth is, not so much any more. I wouldn't have believed that when it first happened, when I was so devastated. What with you coming along, Brian never left my mind. But after . . . after you left . . . it was a different kind of loss. Because, you see, I knew you still existed, you were still in the world. Far away, but reachable."

"Did you ever think — I mean, seriously — of getting me back?"

"Yes. And yet I knew I couldn't do that to Daniel and Katherine — or to you."

"One time I heard Claudine and Daniel talk about your 'tragic romance.' Did they mean Brian or . . . ?"

"Oh, definitely Brian. I was married briefly a few years ago but it didn't work out. With Brian . . . well, I'm sure it would have." Aunt Meg gathered up the things and put them back into the box.

My phone rang. To my "hello" a small voice said, "Is this Lindsay?"

"Arvin! Hey Arvin, how're you doing?"

"Just fine. How're *you* doin'? Is that leg of yours still painin' you?"

"It was. But Arvin, just now, hearing your voice, that old pain melted right away." I shrugged and smiled at Aunt Meg, who smiled back and then left with the box.

"How are your folks?" I asked.

"Why, they're just fine. They went off in the truck to Hartsburg but I couldn't go along 'cause I got me a touch of poison ivy."

"No kidding! Does it hurt?"

"No, it just itches some if I get out in the sun. The reason they said I could call you was to make up for all this sufferin' I'm going through."

"That's really nice." Imagine, me an antidote for poison ivy.

"Well, I guess I'll be sayin' good-bye before I run up the bill sky high. You say hello to Jess for me, now."

"Okay. Bye, Arvin. Hey, kid, come up and visit us some time, will you?"

"Hoooeeee! Wouldn't that be somethin' though!"

"And thanks for calling." I wanted to say, 'I love you,' but I settled for "Take care now!"

Meg came back carrying her purse. "Honey, I'm going to run out and get some champagne for tonight. And flowers. It's going to be one big celebration. Oh . . . and the doctor said I should stop by for some crutches. Is there anything I can get for you?"

"No, thanks. There's something I'd like to get myself, though, when I can hobble around. I want to send presents to Arvin Junior and his parents."

"Fine. They're such a nice family."

"Really. Oh, just to warn you, I'm not going to answer the phone when you're out. I don't want to see or even talk to Jess or Ruthanne before tonight. I'm afraid I might spill the beans."

"Oh, Lindsay." The smile was mostly in her eyes.

"What's the matter? What did I say?"

" 'I might spill the beans.' That's about as American . . . !" She leaned forward and gave me a light kiss on the forehead. "My kid is losing her British accent and expressions." She started to leave, then paused at the door. "You might try to work in a nap. Tonight's going to be a lulu."

"Okay." I snuggled down, lifted the top sheet and let it billow over my body.

I didn't know people dreamed during daytime slumber. I did, though, that day. I was running through fields and then I flung myself down on my back, looked up at the clouds, and caught the scent of flowers all about me.

I opened my eyes. I was lying on my back. I looked up at the ceiling and then sideways. There was a little bouquet of the most delicate flowers I'd ever seen, on my bedside table.

"Sweet peas," Meg said from the doorway. "For sweet dreams and even sweeter awakenings."

"They're marvelous."

"Feel like getting up?"

"Sure. May I get dressed?"

"I don't see why not." She brought over the clothes I indicated. "I saw Ruthanne outside, just for a minute, and headed her off. She knows something is going on but I'm sure she doesn't know *what*."

"Of course she doesn't. If she did it would be on the five o'clock news."

"That's about right. Lean on me, Lin, so you won't put any weight on that leg. Hold on while I tuck in the top and zip the zipper."

The crutches weren't too hard to use. Waiting was the hard part now.

＊

When everyone was there, Meg knew and I knew that there was no way to hold the news until after dinner. There was too much happiness in the air. Ruthanne was like a little kid who couldn't wait to see what was under the tree at Christmas. "Tell me!" she squealed. "I know it's something tremendous! Tell!" Even Jess looked curious.

"I'll get the champagne," Uncle Robert said.

He brought it out, popped the cork, and filled the glasses. "Here's to loved ones, reunited," he said. "After too many years." We all drank a little. "Tell them, Meg," he said.

She did, with smiles and tears. It was really crazy there for a while, with Jess and Ruthanne talking wildly, and everyone laughing and carrying on.

The dinner that night could have been rock-hard frozen, for all the attention anyone paid to the plates.

"Tell me again," Ruthanne said for surely the umpteenth time. "How is it that Lindsay is my cousin? Now, suddenly?"

Jess gave her a withering look. "If you'd listen, instead of yammering all the . . ."

"Hey, Jess," Uncle Robert objected.

Jess looked ceilingward for a second. "Dad and Brian were brothers. Right?"

"Well, they still are brothers," Ruthanne said. "Even though poor Uncle Brian . . ."

"See what I mean?" Jess said.

"Ruthanne, shut up," Uncle Robert said. "Go on, Jess."

"Dad and Brian were brothers. So if Brian was Lindsay's father, then Lindsay and you and I are cousins."

"Well, then, what about Aunt Meg?"

"She's our aunt by marriage."

"And so is Uncle Daniel?"

"No," I broke in. Jess was about to lose his patience again. "Daniel's my real mother's brother, but no relation to you."

"Oh, dear, I don't believe I'll get it all sorted out for a while," Ruthanne said with a sigh.

"Sure you will," I said, And then, "That's a cute top you're wearing. Is it new?" That finally got her off the subject.

I didn't want them to go on about Daniel. He was the one unhappy note in this whole affair. I honestly couldn't dredge up any feelings for Brian, even though he was my birth father. Daniel was something else again. He was the only father I'd ever known, and I wanted him to be that still. I almost dreaded his coming over in a few days. I mean, then I would have to face up to the fact. I didn't know if I could — or how I should act when I saw him.

I needn't have worried. One look at Daniel and I yelled, "Father!" and almost broke my other leg, stumbling toward him on my crutches.

He grabbed me and held me in a huge hug. "My little girl!" he said. "Gosh, I've missed you, punkin'!"

"I've missed you too," I said. "How's everything back home?"

"Fine, fine. They all send their love." His arms suddenly dropped from around me, and as I glanced up I saw his face redden. "Well, Meg, she looks fine," he said, clearing his throat a little.

"Yes, from the knees up, at least," Meg said. Her lips were smiling but her eyes looked frightened. Why? I wondered as I hobbled to a chair. Why?

Then, as they got into the kind of small talk meant to cover up feelings, I realized why. *How's everything back home?* It was natural for me to have asked that. But still . . . *home*. Was it my home? Now?

I didn't know. And as I sat there with the two of them, adding my bit here and there to the cover-up conversation, I knew what was going through their minds. Because it was also going through mine. A choice must be made. Not now, but soon. I could stay on here with my mother. She wanted me, I knew; she'd made that very clear. But she was fair. If I chose to go back with Daniel she wouldn't stand in my way. No one needed to tell me that. I knew it would be my choice. But I didn't want to think about it. Not now.

The next morning, when Meg was getting ready for work, she asked if I wanted someone to come over to stay with me.

"Why? Where's Daniel?"

"He had to go to an early meeting with your Uncle Robert. Did you know they're driving downstate tomorrow, just for the day?"

"Tomorrow! And I don't have the presents!"

"Maybe Janice could take you shopping, if you feel up to it."

"I feel up to it." But after Meg left I called Hope to see if she could take me instead. It was a good way to keep our friendship going, away from Jess.

Hope sounded her old good-spirited self when she picked up the phone. "I've been wanting to get together with you anyway," she said. "Jess sketched out your story, but he didn't go into detail."

"You should have asked Ruthanne."

"She's playing it cagy. My guess is that she's writing it up for some tabloid. Pick you up in an hour."

Hope and I decided to go to the mall because with my cast and crutches it was easier to shop in one building than to get in and out of the car at various village stores.

I got a new Atari cassette for Arvin along with a wild-looking hat and goggles for him to wear on his bike. I got Kim a really cute pair of gold snowflake earrings, hoping her ears were pierced. Arvin's parents stumped me, though.

"How about a cookbook?" Hope asked. "Hey, a wok? And a Chinese cookbook? They could both enjoy those."

"Hope, I don't think so.

"A super picnic basket? With special places for goblets and a bottle of wine?"

"Ho-ope!"

"Those are my best shots. I don't know them like you do."

In a gift department I found something that seemed just right for the Goebberts. It was a really darling ceramic milk pitcher in the shape of a cat, with his tail curled for the handle, and with mugs to match.

Poor Hope was getting a bit bogged down with packages but she said she could take on more, provided they were small.

Small usually means expensive, and the beads I found for Claudine were certainly that. I could see the coral color, though, against her perfect skin, and I had to get them. And for my *ayah*, another bangle, of course.

"I can hardly wait to see the expressions on their faces when . . . uh . . . oh . . ." I stopped.

Hope looked concerned. "Does your leg hurt?"

"It did, just for a moment. I'm okay now." We went on. It wasn't my leg that hurt, though. It was the thought that I probably wouldn't see the looks on Claudine's and my *ayah*'s faces at all. But I could. And that thought hurt just as much.

That night I wrapped the gifts for Arvin and his family. "You won't mind taking these down?" I asked Daniel.

"Not so long as we're driving. No problem." He motioned toward the jewelry boxes. "Aren't you going to wrap those?"

"Uh . . . well, I don't have to, right now." And then because both Daniel and Meg looked puzzled, I took out the beads and bangle. "These are for Claudine and Hamida."

Daniel held up the necklace. "Claudine will be crazy about this," he said. "Coral looks good on her, as you know. But honey, this must have cost a fortune."

"No matter. I made stacks of money, toiling in the fields. And anyway, this is a way of showing Claudine how much . . ." I took the necklace back and made a big thing of arranging it just so in the box.

There was an awkward pause. And there was that question again, hanging in the air.

Suddenly Daniel slapped his hands against his knees. "I could use a drink. How about you girls?"

"Sure," Meg said. "Come on out to the kitchen, Danny, and I'll show you how to mix a margarita."

They left, and I took the jewelry boxes into my bedroom, to get them out of sight. And also out of mind, at least for a little while.

I slumped into my wicker chair, overcome suddenly with longing. A longing to be back in that place of so many memories. A place where life was leisurely. Where the only thing to disturb the quiet of the night was bird song, the hum of overhead fans, and voices drifting in from the servants' quarters. And where devotion was never questioned.

Why couldn't I be there and here as well? Why did one have to make choices? And with a heartbreak either way?

Chapter Nineteen

"Turk," I said to him the next afternoon, "it's really nice of you to drive me all this way to the planetarium. And on your day off from work too."

"I thought you might like a change of surroundings."

"Right. I feel so mired down. Not just because of the cast. It's everything. There's a pressure. But I just can't seem to focus."

"Maybe the sky show will help. Sometimes a new perspective . . ."

"I wish. But staring at the stars won't help me make up my mind. It's so confusing, you know. And either way it's going to hurt."

"Make up your mind about going back or not?"

"Yes." I lifted my cast-heavy leg to ease it a bit. "It's not just the going or staying. It's making a choice. Where are my loyalties, with my mother or my father? I still think of him as *Father*. I guess I always will."

"Has either one said it? Said you should choose?"

"No, but it's there, Turk. The looks on their faces. Father's look is resigned. And sad. Meg's is frightened. But neither one would try to influence me. I know that."

Turk waited for the light to change and turned onto the Outer Drive. "So it's really up to you to decide," he said then.

"Yes, but how can I?"

"Does it have to be that permanent? Couldn't you sort of go back and forth?"

"I could. But I need to *belong*. To be someone's daughter. Their real, true daughter."

"If that's what you need, then it seems to me the choice has been made," he said after a pause.

"I guess." I looked at the flurry of sailboats out on Lake Michigan, vivid colors flung against the blue of the water. "You know, Turk, in a way it isn't fair. She did give me up, after all."

"Do you blame her for that?"

"No, of course not. She hadn't much choice, being so young and all."

"Then what point are you trying to make?"

"Just that Father took me in good faith. Thinking I'd be his always."

"Lindsay, let me tell you something. Nothing is for always. And kids aren't something people *own*. Parents are there to love and protect until the child grows old enough to take care of itself."

"Yes, that's true, but . . ."

"And at best you'll have only a year or so more to be around either of them. Then you'll be off to college and headed for your own life."

"That sounds a bit scary, Turk, being adrift like that." Again my look turned to the boats heading into the wind.

"But you'll always be able to count on your parents. They'll be there . . . both of them . . . if you need some kind of help."

"I suppose." I got out a comb and ran it down inside the cast where my leg itched. "I really want to know my mother better. It'll be different for us now — we can relax and be open with each other. And we do need this time, before I'm grown up and gone." As long as the comb was out I ran it through my hair. "Turk," I said then, tucking the comb back into my purse, "I'm so grateful."

"For what?"

"You've helped me sort it all out. And with just a few little words. Where do you get this absolutely astonishing insight?"

He shrugged. "People who don't fit in develop their own way of looking at things."

"But, Turk, you fit in!" I said, lying.

He shook his head. "No, I don't. Neither do you. That isn't important. It's what goes on inside of you. I figure I'm about six years ahead of myself, compared to other kids. But after I'm grown, I'll slow down and eventually I'll be at the same level as others my age."

I looked at him. "You'll never be on the same level, Turk. You'll always be ahead of the others."

Turk half smiled. "You're probably right," he admitted. "But so will you."

"Bingo!" I said.

The subject of *Lindsay, make up your mind* never did come up. My father, always uncomfortable when it came to expressing feelings, simply didn't raise the issue. But he could tell. The knowledge grew in his eyes as I began (a cowardly move on my part) talking of plans for high school in the fall. And any vague doubt was dispelled when I gave him the gifts to take back to India.

"Please be sure to tell Claudine I love and miss her," I said, "and the same to Hamida." Then, with an attempt at lightness, I went on: "If you happen to meet Rajee tell him I'm doing marvelously well, and am constantly pursued by hordes of love-crazed guys." Finally, as an afterthought, I said, "Just don't mention my broken leg and crutches. That would blow the image."

I honestly did try to talk to Father, to tell him how I felt about him and how I'd always regard him as a true parent. But whenever I did, he'd squirm, pat my hand, and make some excuse to change the subject. Finally I gave up.

The night before he left he kissed me good night several times. "Be good to Meg," he told me. "I tried to take good care of you for her."

"You did take good care of me. But I'm going to miss you, Father." I started crying. "Why does it have to be this way? Us here and you 'way over there?"

"Robert and his family came back. So may we, one of these years."

"But until then?"

He put his arm around me. "I've tried to talk Meg and Eliot into coming over for their honeymoon. They don't know about India, but I think we can convince them to get as far as Greece or Italy."

"What does that have to do with . . . ?"

"They'll bring you along, of course."

"On their honeymoon? Really, Father!"

"They'd do it. What the heck. We could all meet somewhere or other. And then you could fly on and stay with us for a while."

"You mean it? Oh, Dad!"

"*Dad,* is it now? Fancy that." He laughed. "It's time I left . . . before I become *Pop.*"

I didn't know that his good-night kiss was also for good-bye. He was gone the next morning when I woke up. It was Saturday and Meg was home.

"But *why?*" I wailed. "Why couldn't we have said a proper good-bye?" His breakfast dishes were still in the sink.

"He said it would hurt too much. It was better this way. I don't know that I agree, but then . . ." She handed me an envelope and a little box. "He left these for you."

I opened the box. It was a gold ring set with a ruby. "Is this," I asked her, "something he bought to take the place of Rajee's ring?" I had sent that back.

"I don't think so, Lin. He brought this with him before he even knew about Rajee."

I opened the note and read:

> *Dearest Lindsay:*
>
> *I write this with a certain amount of sadness because I know our days of being together as father and daughter have come to a close. Yet, you will always be the daughter of my heart. I've loved you through the years and will continue to look upon you with love and pride as you grow into the wonderful woman I know you will be.*
>
> *Keep a warm place in your heart for me and know that I will never be faraway in thoughts and in love. I wish I could say these things in person but words don't come easily to me when they touch the heart.*
>
> *Look after yourself and look after your mother. Show her that I have kept you well.*
>
> > *Love always,*
> > *Father*

Oh, Father, you *can* express your feelings, I thought. In your own quiet, private way.

Eyes brimming with tears, I looked up, but Meg had

gone. She'd sensed that I needed these moments alone, for mourning. I leaned forward on the table and sobbed. I cried not only for my father, but for the days that were gone and would never return.

As time went on it no longer seemed necessary to cling to Jess. The natural bond of being related was enough to hold us together.

My other friendships took an upward turn.

"Lindsay," a girl said one evening as a bunch of us were driving to a party, "you seem so different these days."

"Different from what?" I asked.

"You're not as weird."

"Sure I am. I'm just weird in the same way you are now. That's why you wouldn't notice."

"No kidding, though. You don't talk funny anymore and you're not always show . . . uh . . ."

"Showing off?"

"Well . . ."

Turk spoke up. "Lindsay never did show off. She was only reflecting her past life . . . the way she was raised. You shouldn't blame her for that."

"I guess. It must have been scary for you, Lindsay, being thrown in with a whole bunch of kids you didn't know, and feeling strange and foreign and out of place and all."

"It was scary, all right," I said lightly. "But to me, you guys were the foreigners and strange. Real strange."

"Fancy that!" the girl said with a British accent. All of us laughed. And then the subject was dropped.

I do feel more and more at home. Most of the time I'm too busy, too involved with the present, to think of, much less yearn for, the past.

Now and then, though, before sleep comes, I drift back

183

in memory to the other times. But gradually these reveries are fading, like madras cloth left in the sun too long.

Some day, I'm sure, I'll take up travel again. I'll visit my father and Claudine, and possibly visit new places too. But only for a while.

As I said in a congratulatory letter I finally decided to write to Rajee:

> *Perhaps some day our paths will cross again. But as for now, I'm most content to be in the country that claims me. And with my mother, who could never quite give up her claim.*

Just writing those words gave me a tremendous feeling of peace.

I'm the same Lindsay as ever I was. But at last I've found my place. I'm back where I'm loved, where I belong. I'm home.